Jaymar Jackson

Copyright © 2024 by Jamaris Jackson.

All rights reserved. No part of this publication may be reproduced, distributed, or transmitted in any form or by any means, including photocopying, recording, or other electronic or mechanical methods, without the prior written permission of the publisher, except in the case of brief quotations embodied in critical reviews and certain other noncommercial uses permitted by copyright law.

ISBN 979-8-9900386-2-2

Published by Jamaris Jackson

Printed in United States

For permission requests, contact the publisher at tceseries2024@gmail.com

Visit tceseries.com for additional information about this book and the author.

First Edition: February 2024

10 9 8 7 6 5 4 3 2 1

Dedicated to My People,

From Black to Brown to Beige,

We are most powerful when we unite,

Rather than finding reasons to divide.

For those who feel unseen,

For those who feel unheard,

For those who feel alone,

For those who feel the pressure to be perfect,

For those who feel lost,

This is for you.

-Jaymar

Table of Contents

Prologue 1

Chapter 1: In the Beginning, There Was Ray 3

Chapter 2: Issa Turn Up Sis 14

Chapter 3: Bro Bro, Leh Go 25

Chapter 4: What the Hell?! 34

Chapter 5: Celestial Revelations 47

Chapter 6: Elemental Beginnings 79

Chapter 7: Demon Time 99

Chapter 8: Highs and Lows 114

Chapter 9: Drinks, Desperations and... Demons?! 135

Chapter 10: Something Wicked This Way... 151

Chapter 11: Fade to Black 169

Chapter 12: Down in the Dark 190

Chapter 13: Into the Light 200

Chapter 14: The Grey Area 213

Prologue

From a vantage point beyond any mortal perception, the Devil reclines upon his throne, surrounded by a legion of demons. In the sprawling abyss, pits of hellfire cast an eerie glow, perpetually fueling the screams of tormented souls in a cacophony of agony and despair. Before him stand his generals, embodiments of the seven deadly sins, awaiting his words.

"For centuries," the Devil begins, his voice a low, chilling rumble that reverberates through the sulfurous air, "God and I have waged our battle through our loyal servants." He addresses the assembly of sin, eyes ablaze with an infernal glow. "Every five centuries, he deploys a team of young warriors to thwart us, maintaining a fragile equilibrium. But lately, our dominion has flourished. Earth has become a wellspring, an influx of souls swelling our domain. It is time for you to rise once more, my faithful emissary ..."

In that moment, a tall, shadowy figure emerges from the Devil's right side, converging into a form. Standing at seven feet, a sinister smile playing across his features, the demon exudes an aura that could subdue the strongest will to quivering submission.

"Jonathan Caine, my right hand," the Devil pronounces, his voice resonating with dark authority, "it is time for you to claim the souls of Earth once more, conserve my reign." His gaze fixates on Caine. "We have savored centuries of anguish and pain, courtesy of a fatal error by one of their warriors. Your task is to sustain this energy flow into my dominion. You must defeat his six warriors once again."

"I will not falter, Master," Caine asserts, his voice laced with conviction. "We shall thrive, and I shall vanquish God's warriors once more."

Lucifer, like a paternal figure, grips Caine's shoulder, a gesture of dark camaraderie. "A toast," he exclaims, his voice a chilling echo amid the screams. "To my right hand! May he herald centuries of torment and chaos upon our enemies, in the name of all that is unholy!" Amid the tumult, cheers and jubilation resonate, an ominous celebration that reverberates throughout the furthest reaches of the infernal domain. Evil, undeniably, was on the rise.

Chapter 1: In the Beginning, There Was Ray

It is a bright, warm Sunday morning. A young Black boy is sitting in church, clapping, and enjoying a rendition of "This Little Light of Mine." His mother sings in the choir as he sits next to his grandmother.

Suddenly, the boy's mother stops swaying with the choir and looks directly at him, the music abruptly stops. A look of worry overcomes the boy's face. He stands up. He looks around to see the entire congregation staring at him, feeling his anxiety creep across his nerves as it begins to heighten. He turns back to his mother; she and the choir are gone.

He then experiences a sense of abandonment around him, he turns to look back and the congregation is gone as well. He is racked with worry and fear. The light outside slowly evaporates and darkness envelopes the air. Clanging of metal and shrieking can be heard from outside. The young boy walks slowly toward the church doors, he turns the knob and opens the doors.

A desolate, familiar land is before the young boy. The air is murky and stale. Disfigured, lifeless, and charred bodies litter the landscape, reminiscent of a graveyard amid the haunting resemblance of a war-torn zone. A band of warriors are standing on a precipice and looking down at an army draped in black and red.

There is a general giving a command for his forces to attack, they follow their orders. The warriors, propelled by determination, swiftly spring into action, engaging in a fierce clash with the mysterious, shadowy adversaries.

The atmosphere reverberates with the howl of wind, crackling lightning, and the tumultuous rush of water, while the earth quakes and fractures, engulfed by blazing fires that spiral and surge. Amid the chaos, a streak of ominous black light pierces the battleground, swiftly followed by an intense, radiant white brilliance that floods the entire expanse, engulfing all in its blinding embrace.

The scene of the desolate battlefield shatters like a broken mirror, and suddenly, Raymond finds himself jolted from that haunting space into the familiar comfort of his own bedroom. His heart races, confusion lingering in the wake of the surreal experience. As he scans the room, his eyes graze over the familiar posters, the remnants of a typical life for a young, nerdy Black boy. "I really gotta stop eating wings after eleven," he mutters, shaking off the residual unease that clings to his skin.

With a groan, he rises from his bed, disturbing his dog, Wott, who lazily acknowledges the morning's intrusion before curling back into sleep. He throws the sheets off his body and reluctantly stumbles out of bed into the bathroom.

Ray is your typical twenty-eight-year-old young Black man. He stands at six foot three, espresso complexion, a large nose, brown eyes and a bald head accented with a beard. Born in a rural city in Alabama he graduated from the University of Alabama; then moved to Atlanta ... like every other person who wanted to start a music career.

He goes into the kitchen and pours a bowl of cereal and checks the morning news. He later brushes his teeth and starts up the shower, he imagines his life on tour and performing in front of thousands. Ray always wanted a career in music. It had been his dream ever since he was ten. He moved to Atlanta after he graduated college because he had a job lined up, but he really wanted to start his music career. "I can't control the feeling!" sings Ray as he stands in the shower imitating one of his favorite artists, Maxwell. He finishes up in the shower, grabs a towel, walks back into his bedroom and checks his phone (no new texts). "And that's my life," he scoffs as he throws the phone back onto the bed.

Ray then searches his chest and dresser drawers for clothes to wear for the day. He isn't going anywhere for the moment; he works from home for a tech company so he can watch his dog during the day. He logs on to his computer and starts up his applications. He then calls into a meeting where everyone is discussing their daily tasks.

Ray daydreaming again, misses hearing his name being called. "Yo Ray Dog!" screams Ray's irritating coworker breaking his train of thought. He knows Ray hates it when they urbanize his name, the typical macro-aggressions of the tech work environment.

"Yea, Will, what's up?" Ray replies in a begrudging tone.

"How are those two tasks coming along?" asks Will.

"They are finished and I have moved them to quality assurance testing," replies Ray sure of his own hard work.

"Greaaaaattttt," replies Will, ready to reply with an unwelcome request. "That means you can take on this extra task before the end of the workday today, right?"

"Will... ," counters Ray, rolling his eyes, "it's Friday evening and we're off tomorrow, that means that I would have to finish this all by this evening."

"Yeah ... I know, but I know you can do it, it should be really easy for you, right?"

If it's so damn easy, why don't you pull out your laptop and do it, thinks Ray.

"C'mon, Ray, pleaseeeeee. The business partners really need this for the next release," says Will begging.

"Alright, sure... I'll take it," Ray says, regretting the decision.

"Atta boy!" exclaims Will.

Ray places the computer microphone on mute. "Don't call me boy, you absent-minded, narrow behind, higher-up, kiss ass!" bellows Ray feeling his emotions flare. He hears the call ending and proceeds to view the task. "This is gonna be one of those days ..." Ray sighs.

Hours later he completes the task and checks the time. "Hmph, guess I should go to the store," he says remembering that the fridge is empty. He throws on a jacket and a pair of shoes. He also remembers to let Wott out into the backyard to let loose. He checks his phone before calling him back into the house and has one message from his mom. Hey, how are you? He ignores the message and lets his dog back in and sends him back to his bed so that he can leave. Ray then proceeds to the garage after grabbing his wallet and phone.

Ray heads out toward the market. He's waiting for a response from another job opportunity, but he knows that he probably won't hear back. He motions down Northside Drive taking in views of the Georgia Aquarium and the Mercedes-Benz Stadium and smiles. As he drives, he signals for an elderly woman to merge in front of him so that she doesn't have to wait.

He begins to think about that dream and what it means. The emotions he felt in that dream begin to surface. He hasn't seen any recent anime that would've triggered a dream like that. A car horn intervenes and Ray snaps out of thought just in time for him to hit his brakes to avoid a car accident. He signals apologies to the other driver. Ray has always had these moments where he envisions himself fighting evil and saving the world, it was something he did from time to time to escape the troubles of the real world, but this dream was different. OK, I gotta pay more attention, he thinks to himself.

Ray pulls into the grocery store's parking lot, the engine's growl fading as he switches off the ignition. Stepping out of his truck, he catches sight of a commotion by the store's entrance. Three figures clustered by the right side, their voices carrying through the air.

His eyes narrow as he observes the tense exchange. Two guys, draped in typical swagger, direct barbs at a third, their words laced with mockery. "Hey, man, nice look you got there," one taunts with a sneer, eyeing the unconventional appearance of the distressed young man.

The atmosphere is thick with discomfort as the verbal assault continues. "You tryna to be an anime character or something?" jibes the other, relishing in the discomfort he was causing.

"I-I don't want any trouble," stutters the distressed figure, his voice trembling with fear.

Before the situation could escalate further, Ray marches over, his voice booming with authority. "Hey, what's goin' on?"

The two troublemakers spin around, their bravado crumbling as Ray's towering presence looms over them. Their confident smirks falter into panicked expressions, and without a word, they hastily retreat, leaving behind a palpable sense of relief in their wake.

Ray turns his attention to the distressed young man, his tone reassuring. "Looks like they won't be bothering you anymore."

As Ray glances back, he notices the previously distressed figure sprinting away in the opposite direction, fleeing the scene with a mixture of gratitude and haste. Ray stands confused for a moment and then pushes on. He grabs a cart and proceeds into the store to shop. While he is shopping, he helps a young boy grab cereal off a high shelf. The other half of the dream he had begins to play in his head. While he's daydreaming, he is interrupted by a familiar voice.

"You know you STAY daydreamin'," says the voice. "That's probably why you can't get any real work done."

It was Ray's coworker Qasim. Qasim was twenty-seven, six foot four, green eyes, low haircut, honey skin complexion, with a muscular build and a smile that could light up even the darkest of corners of the earth.

"Ha, you are the one who needs to be checking their work ethic, I've seen your task board," says Ray. They dap up and Ray talks about how the team doesn't realize how hard the developers have it.

Qasim laughs it off and then rattles on about their team member Kianna, and how thick she is. Qasim has a one-track mind and girls were at the end of that track. "That's really all you think about, huh, man?" says Ray side-eyeing Qasim.

"What else is there to think about?" questions Qasim confirming Ray's query. Ray shakes his head and he and Qasim continue to walk through the grocery store.

Again, Ray's dream interrupts his thoughts. He stares off into space, enveloped in a sense of wonder and worry. He feels his breath beginning to pace faster and his eyes begin to dart. His mind races with the images from the dream.

"Ray, Raaaaayyyyy ... Ray!" exclaims Qasim. Ray snaps out of his trance back into reality. The smell of the grocery store bringing him slowly back to Qasim's presence.

"Huh?!"

Qasim laughs. "I was asking you, what were you doing tonight?"

"Oh, me?!" Ray looks down at the basket with one bottle of Prosecco and ingredients for a Rotel dip. "Nothing, nothing at all, what's up?" says Ray unconvincingly.

"So, there's this party tonight one of my neos is hosting, you wanna go?" asks Qasim putting his fist to his palm.

"Ain't they like twenty and twenty-one? I'm not tryna be caught up in any jail time when the cops come to the dorm," replies Ray worrying about the potential for being incarcerated.

Qasim chuckles. "Well, it's at their off-campus house and they're checking ID, no one under twenty-one gets to drink. C'mon, man, you ain't doing nothing tonight."

I'm not, Ray thought to himself. "OK, I'm down, I'll roll with you," says a reluctant Ray.

"Cool, I'll send you the address and meet you there, now you can put back that bottle of Prosecco," says Qasim as he smiles and walks away.

"I'm still gonna buy it!" exclaims Ray as he continues to shop. He walks down the chip aisle for Tostitos. He notices an elderly man staring at him and Ray turns away. As soon as he turns back to address him, he is gone. He goes for the Tostitos but finds that there is already a bag of them in his cart. Ray adopts a confused look on his face and ponders why he feels a strange and strong connection to the man who was there.

Chapter 2: Issa Turn Up Sis

"'Watch out, V!" exclaims Khalia, hastily calling out to her best friend as they share the volleyball court.

"I got it, sis!" exclaims Viera. As a volleyball speeds toward Viera, she motions for a strike. With her adrenaline pumping and a heavy breath, she jumps into action in a split second. She leaps into the air, pulls her hand back, and in the perfect moment, hits the ball for a perfect spike in the open defense. "YES!" screams Viera.

A whistle blows. "Point, set, match!" notes the referee. Cheers erupt, marking their triumph as the referee officially declares the game's end.

Their victory sends ripples of excitement through the crowd. Viera's heart still pounds with the thrill of that final spike, the moment when everything aligned perfectly—a culmination of practice, focus, and determination. Khalia's cheers echo in her ears, adding to the jubilation. They high-five other teammates, sharing the elation of their win. The taste of victory lingers in the air, the culmination of their teamwork and unspoken understanding on the court.

"Oh my God, girl, that's a crazy game!" exclaims Viera, wiping the sweat off her brow.

"Yeah, but you always pull it off, sis!" exclaims Khalia.

"I try, girl, I try!" Viera and Khalia exchange spirited praise for each other's efforts as they make their way from the court to the locker room.

Viera feels a surge of pride and accomplishment, her eyes meeting Khalia's, exchanging a glance filled with unspoken camaraderie. The court remains a canvas where they weave their athletic prowess, each move a testament to their friendship and shared passion for the game. As they step off the court, the thrill of victory follows them, etching another memorable chapter in their journey as friends and athletes.

Viera Adams and Khalia Brown are best friends who attend Spelman University, they've been friends since freshman year. Viera, at twenty-two, a vision of determination, aspires to revolutionize special education, dreaming of founding her own school for children with special needs. Her five-foot-nine frame, amber eyes, sand-colored skin, and a distinct mole on her left cheek complement her fiery spirit. Khalia, a year younger, stands tall at five foot ten, her bronze complexion and light brown eyes adding to her confident demeanor. A political science major with limited ambitions to follow her mother's esteemed legal career, Khalia epitomizes intelligence and resilience.

The warm Atlanta evening beckons as they discuss plans for the night. Khalia eagerly proposes a party hosted by Zeke and Trelle, but Viera hesitates, citing her responsibilities toward her sisters and upcoming tests. "Hey, Zeke and Trelle are having a party tonight, you down?" asks Khalia.

"Hmm, I don't know, girl …," questions Viera, "I gotta check on my sisters and make sure they're good and I got a test next Tuesday I need to study for and—"

"Girl, stop, you're going. You're always trying to take care of them," interrupts Khalia. "What about you for a change?"

"Girl, what am I supposed to do? You know how my mama is!" rebuts Viera.

"Look I'll get you a sitter online and that way y'all both can go out," resolves Khalia.

Eventually, Viera relents, agreeing to meet Khalia later. "OK, girl, I'll meet you there tonight."

"EOOOWWWWWW!" exclaims Khalia. "How 'bout I pick you up at nine instead?!"

"OK cool, I'll spot you for gas money," replies Viera.

"Girl, bye!" exclaims Khalia as she closes her car door and drives off.

As Khalia revs the engine of her sleek new Range Rover and speeds away, Viera lingers beside her trusty 2009 Toyota Camry. A soft sigh escapes her lips, a wistful longing surfacing as she allows her mind to wander into a realm of dreams and aspirations. Standing there, she conjures a vivid vision of herself, comfortably seated behind the wheel of her own car, an embodiment of her future aspirations.

Viera was always a bit envious of Khalia even though they're best friends. Khalia's mother works as a powerful attorney in Atlanta; she has worked on some notable cases, many with high monetary outcomes and her father is a computer engineer for a major tech company. Khalia's family has never truly had to go without. "One day ..." Viera sighs as she enters her car and drives off.

She later arrives home, a small townhome nestled in the middle of a block of houses in downtown Atlanta. The sense of responsibility clings to her, as natural as her next breath. "Keisha! Kimber! I'm home!" she exclaims, signaling her sisters to enter the living room.

Viera is greeted by her younger twin sisters, Keisha and Kimber, born nine years after her. They scurry into the room, each displaying their distinct personalities. "Hey, sis!" they exclaim in unison.

Despite the weariness of the day, her thoughts drift to her sisters' well-being. "What do you guys want for dinner tonight?" Viera questions, scrolling through a delivery app.

"I want something fun," says Kimber, hanging on the edge of the couch.

"It does not matter to me," replies Keisha, turning on the television and opening the Netflix app.

"How about pizza?" Viera responds, eager to indulge their joy.

"Yes!" the twin sisters exclaim with enthusiasm.

Viera chuckles. "Alright, let me get on it."

Viera locates the local pizza delivery restaurant, her mind partially wandering as she looks out of the screen door of their home. Across the street, she notices a man in a strange garment staring at her. She steps out, intending to address him, but a passing diesel truck startles her, causing her to lose focus. By the time the truck passes, the man has vanished, leaving her perplexed and unnerved. "OK, yeah, it's been a long day," she laments, brushing off the momentary unease. She closes the door and turns back to her sisters. "Hey, did Mama say when she'd get back?"

"No, she just said to make sure we was fed and that she'd be back when she won big," says Kimber, mimicking their mother's voice.

"Of course, she did," sighs Viera. "And Kimber, it's 'were,' not 'was.' You're not a baby anymore; you know your grammar."

"Ugh, OK," responds Kimber, a mix of amusement and resignation in her voice.

* * *

Meanwhile, in Brookhaven, Khalia arrives at her lavish home, calling out for her parents but receiving no response. "Momma?! Daddy?!" she exclaims. No one responds.

"Hmm... I guess they're both still at work," she ponders. "Maybe I can sneak into Dad's lab." She walks toward the back of the house, quickly picking up momentum. Khalia isn't your typical wealth-driven socialite. She's very thankful for the things that she has, but she's not interested in material things.

Khalia is actually vastly intelligent with a secret passion for all things technological. Her father is lead hardware engineer for a big-name tech company that focuses on communications. Khalia makes her way down to her father's lab, turns on the lights and begins examining the room. Her father's workstation is compact, humming with innovation. She strides toward an active, unlocked workstation, the screen casting a soft glow in the dimly lit room.

"Let's see what Dad has been working on," says Khalia as she begins rapidly tapping the keyboard exploring files and analyzing lines of code algorithms.

"Oh wow! These are schematics for an interchangeable clothing system that's built into a smartwatch ... this could—"

"Khalia! Where are you, dear?!" Khalia's mom's voice fills the large mansion until it reaches the technology laboratory.

"Ah damn!" Khalia scrambles to get her flash drive, inserts it into the computer and copies the data over to it. She exits the door just before her mother sees her and makes a motion to appear that she's coming from the bathroom. "Hey, Mama, what's up?"

"Hey, honey, have you studied for your political science exam Monday?" asks her mom putting away groceries with a concerned demeanor.

"Oh yeah... About that... I kinda... forgot," Khalia says while rubbing the back of her neck.

"Oh, c'mon now, Lia, I talked to your professor and he says that you have the capacity to learn it; you're just not trying to make it

21

happen," says Khalia's mom deeply concerned with her daughter's lack of concern for her classes.

"And I appreciate you getting me the makeup exam, Mama, look ima get into it don't worry!" explains Khalia grabbing an apple while moving backward toward the staircase to the next floor.

"You said that when you took the first exam," scoffs Khalia's mom, placing her hands on the counter and wincing at her daughter.

"Ma, I promise you I got it," says Khalia as she motions her way toward and up the stairs.

"I really hope so," says Khalia's mom as she turns her attention back to the groceries.

Khalia makes her way to her bedroom and closes the door. "Whew, that was a close one!" Khalia's room is lined with posters of '90s movies and icons. She makes her way over to her computer and inserts the flash drive with her dad's data in and connects her smartwatch to the computer as well.

Multiple screens open and she begins clicking away. "Hmm, this is almost complete. Just missing a few things ...," says Khalia as she completes the algorithm. "Got it!" The mouse she is using short circuits just as she finishes clicking and the lights flicker. She goes to check to see if the house across the street is having a similar problem. She looks out her window down at the driveway and sees a man standing there in eclectic clothing. He is staring directly into her window with a piercing glare.

Khalia hears her mother walking up the stairs and switches her laptop screen to a browser. "Hey, Ma, you expecting anybody?" She looks away from the window and walks toward the door.

"No, dear, why?" replies Khalia's mom with a concerned look.

"There's a guy outside looking up into my room!" exclaims a fearful Khalia.

"What?!" gasps Khalia's mom. She and Khalia walk over to the window and examine the driveway and see nothing there. "Khalia, is this a joke?!" questions Khalia's mom deeply concerned.

"No, Mama, somebody was out there!" replies Khalia racked with confusion.

"OK, I'll check the cameras." Khalia knows someone is standing there watching her. She can't help but wonder who the man is.

Chapter 3: Bro Bro, Leh Go

Two young men, clad in purple and black, distribute flyers near Piedmont Park. Ezekiel, one of them, confidently approaches a passerby, attempting to entice her to their upcoming party.

"Aye, lil' mama, wait, wait now, slow down. Look the bruhs and I are having a party tonight and the turn-up is gonna be real; now c'mon ... I know you down!" says Ezekiel, deploying his charisma.

"Honey, I am twenty-seven, I ain't going to no frat party!" says the young woman as she begins walking away.

Undeterred, Ezekiel employs his charm, assuring her of the event's maturity and allure. "Wait a minute now, miss, I am very sorry to disturb you, but you have to understand something," explains Ezekiel, attempting to soften her stance. "Now you may think we're just a couple of young, dumb boys who are just horny and all over the place, but I can promise you; if you make your way to our soirée, we can show just how mature we can truly be."

The woman surprisingly giggles and relaxes her demeanor. "Well, since you put it that way, I'll come and I'll let my girlfriends know about the soirée as well," she promises with a chuckle in her voice.

"Great, see YOU tonight," says Ezekiel with a coy smile and a seductive voice.

The woman walks away, and Ezekiel walks up to his best friend, Dontrelle, and daps him up. "AHHHH, Zeke the freak strikes again!" he exclaims, gloating, pride evident in his voice.

"Man, I honestly can't believe that works damn near every time," says Dontrelle, failing to understand how Ezekiel gets away with any of his shenanigans.

"Aye, man, what can I say? When you got the sauce, you just got the sauce!" exclaims Ezekiel, patting his chest for a display of machismo. Dontrelle and Ezekiel both attend Morehouse College in Atlanta. As members of a fraternal organization, they work more on the societal aspect of the organization rather than the communal area. Dontrelle is twenty-three, he stands at about six foot one with a slim/muscular build, beige skin, Afro, and brown eyes. Ezekiel is also twenty-three, standing at five eleven with a similar body build, almond skin, large ears, a fade haircut, and hazel eyes.

Their fraternity is having a party to kick off the new school year. Even though some students are too young to participate, the majority of them will be there. They are working to get others to come, since the house is off-campus.

Ezekiel gets a text from his mother. "Aww damn, man!" exclaims Zeke, slightly flustered by the idea presented to him. "My mama said I need to invite my brother tonight, great."

Dontrelle reassures him, "It ain't no problem, just invite him; he'll hang out with us."

"Man, why you always defending him? He's the older brother; my mama should be sending those texts his way!" Zeke expresses his frustration with the family dynamics.

"Zeke, it doesn't matter, man," says Dontrelle. "There's gonna be enough girls there to take your mind off anybody else, don't worry about it."

"Yeah, you're right, man, the turn-up will commence," says Zeke ecstatically.

Out of the corner of his eye, Dontrelle can see a man standing and watching them from the bushes. "Aye, Zeke, you know that dude?" Dontrelle ponders.

"What dude?" Zeke replies, confused about where to look.

"That dude!" exclaims Dontrelle as he moves Zeke's head from his phone to the man standing and staring at them both. "Aye, yo, can we help you?" asks Dontrelle. The man continues to stare, not moving an inch and not saying a word.

"Aye, man, you got a problem?!" exclaims Zeke, losing his patience with the silence between the two parties. They both walk over to approach the man. Suddenly, a large group of female runners goes by, and Zeke loses his train of thought. "Daaaaammmnnnn, hey, ladies, wait a minute!" yells Zeke, trying to chase down the small group of women.

As the group runs by, Dontrelle loses track of the man while attempting to get Ezekiel to pay attention. Dontrelle turns back to continue addressing the elderly man, and he is gone. "I know ... I'm not ... losin' it ...," says Dontrelle, standing there perplexed. He knew he saw a man standing there, but how could he be there one second and gone the next?

"Yo, Trelle! Come here, I need some flyers!" exclaims Zeke from the other side of the park, distracted by the group of runners, trying to persuade them to join the party that night as well.

"Aight, man, I'm comin'!" exclaims Dontrelle. Dontrelle trips on a piece of elevated ground that looks as though it has just been forced up. He looks around once more before rushing off to help out Zeke. After they pass out the remaining flyers, they head home. On the way, they stop and get things for the party. Alcohol, alcohol, and more alcohol. They arrive home and start unloading the car. "I don't know, man, that didn't seem a little weird to you?" asks Trelle, carrying a crate of liquor into the house.

"Bruh, there are plenty of homeless people who live in the park," says Zeke, helping him. "He was just probably high or somethin', man."

"If you say so," says Dontrelle, walking into the house and shaking his head at Zeke's disbelief.

Trelle and Zeke share a spacious three-bedroom, two-bathroom townhouse, a convenient arrangement rented from Zeke's parents. Their decision to live together stemmed from their deep bond as line brothers, the closest within their fraternity's lineage. What's most interesting is their stark contrast in personalities, almost like two ends of a spectrum coming together under one roof.

Zeke is a bit of a slob and narrow-minded. Zeke has always felt like the wayward stepchild of his family. He feels that his parents are harder on him than they ever were with his brother. Zeke is majoring in African American studies, and he uses the knowledge of what he thinks he's learned in class and applies it to his life. He's obviously a ladies' man who has a knack for always saying the right thing at the right time to get the girl of the moment.

Dontrelle however, is patient and somewhat stoic. He's had a different life than Ezekiel, due to the fact that he was very sheltered as a child, he tends to be more level-headed and quieter from time to time.

While they start to gather everything for the party, Zeke gets a call from his mom. "Hey,

Ma, what's up?" asks Zeke, trying to move furniture and talk at the same time.

"Hey, honey, did you invite your brother to your party tonight?" asks Zeke's mom.

"Yes, Mama." Zeke sighs deeply and rolls his eyes.

"Oh, Zeke, I wish you two were closer like in the old days, what happened to you two? You had such a strong bond," expresses Zeke's mom.

"Ma, we just grew out of each other. It's nothing personal for real, for real, we just ... different now!" exclaims Zeke as he pushes the couch against the wall.

She sighs heavily. "Well, hopefully tonight you guys can turn things around and get back to old times!"

"Yeah, maybe, listen, Ma, I gotta go help Trelle set up for the party tonight. OK, I'll call you later bye!"

"OK, honey, I'll—" Before she could finish, Zeke hangs up the phone and flings it onto the couch.

Dontrelle turns to Zeke and gives a disappointing look.

"Aye, man, don't look at me like that, you know how I feel about him," expresses Zeke.

"I'm gonna look at you like that and you know why I'm looking at you. Stop rushing her off the phone like that, Zeke," says Trelle in an even tone scoring that the way Zeke rushed his mother off the phone was disrespectful.

"Man, she was talking about him, and I don't want to talk about him," explains Zeke.

"Look, man, I understand but that's still ya mama, you only get one," protests Trelle.

"Yeah, man, whatever you say, you don't even know."

As Zeke walks away, Dontrelle's thoughts drift to memories of his own mother, a cherished presence in his life. Her excitement over his admission to Morehouse lingers vividly in his mind. It was the last joyous moment he shared with her before the tragic accident that robbed him of both his parents.

With no other family to turn to, Dontrelle, merely eighteen at the time, found solace in his acceptance to college. Zeke's family generously embraced him until they both settled into their freshman dorm.

Though the weight of these memories pulls at Dontrelle's heart, he refocuses on the party preparations. Soon enough, Zeke rejoins him, lending a hand to ensure everything is ready.

Chapter 4: What the Hell?!

As the night descends, a lively parade of guests floods the party, transforming the once-quiet house into a hub of animated conversations and pulsating beats. The air shakes with the rhythmic thud of music, audible even from a distance as cars approach the driveway.

Inside, a lively atmosphere envelops the space. Laughter intermingles with the melodies, bodies swaying to the tunes, and the ambiance vibrating with an infectious energy. Conversations weave in and out, intertwining with the rhythm of the music as people relish the contagious euphoria of the gathering.

Zeke and Trelle, assuming their roles as experienced hosts, assign their younger members the task of gatekeeping, ensuring entry with a quick check at the door and the distribution of wristbands to those yet to reach the legal drinking age. They oversee the proceedings, ensuring the night unfolds smoothly and responsibly for all attendees.

Khalia and Viera soon pull up to the party, parking and stepping out of Khalia's Range Rover. "Woo! Thanks for getting a babysitter, girl, this is about to be one fun night!" exclaims a thankful Viera.

"You already know it, sis! I'm just ready to shake this stress!" replies an already buzzed Khalia.

"Girl, don't you have a makeup exam Monday?!" questions Viera, tilting her head and squinting her eyes.

Khalia, slightly slurring her speech, says, "Hey, if you won't talk about it, I won't. Leh go!"

Both girls are dressed quite fashionably for the evening. Khalia incorporates a '90s flare into her outfit, and Viera has a modern take on her attire. As the girls approach and enter the house, they are met with greetings and cat calls from the guys surrounding the area. They brush it off and enter.

Around this time, Ray pulls up and gives Qasim a call. The phone rings. Qasim answers. "Aye, man, what's up?" asks Qasim slurring his speech.

"Aye, man, where are you?" Ray's voice crackles with concern as he scans the surroundings. "I'm pullin' up right now, where you at? I'm already here, sitting in the driveway."

"Man, bruh, you such a homebody, get out and go in there!" exclaims Qasim, with his frat brothers encouraging Ray in the background.

"Man, I hate going into a function by myself, especially when all the people there are younger than me," explains Ray. "I feel like a dad coming to take away the fun."

"Well, you're gonna have to go in 'cause I lied, I'm still at home getting ready with the bruhs."

Ray sighs and throws his head back. "When are you gonna be here?" asks Ray impatiently.

"Prolly in the next twenty... thirty minutes," replies Qasim in a questionable tone.

A familiar feeling starts to overcome Ray's conscience and nervousness overtakes his body. He feels this way whenever he thinks people are watching him or staring at him; he always seems to be the biggest person in the room, a focal point. Ray exits the truck and proceeds to walk toward the house. A group of girls walk by, and he tenses up as they giggle together. Even though they aren't talking about him, he feels like they are. He approaches the door and reaches for the handle.

"Oh! Hold up, bruh, I need to see some ID," says the frat member to Ray.

"Oh my bad, bruh," says Ray nervously as he reaches for his ID and shows it. He feels all the eyes of the guys outside staring at him.

"Aight, man, you good, enjoy," affirms the young man at the door as he marks Ray's hand.

Ray walks in and observes the scene. Everyone is really enjoying themselves. Again, he feels like the giant in the room, even though this time no one is watching. He squeezes his way through the crowd, consistently saying excuse me to everyone for brushing up against them. He finds an area where people are vibing to music and sits next to a young man who is seemingly similar in age.

"Hey, anybody sitting here?" asks Ray. The young man shakes his head, and Ray takes a seat. He scans the room again and looks for Qasim; he still hasn't arrived. This was typical of

Qasim. He was late to work, of course, he's late to everything else. Ray stops scanning and turns his attention to the quiet young man next to him. He has his head deep into his phone, trying to avoid contact. He seems to be about six foot with a slender body, although it's hard to gauge his height, almond skin, large ears, high top fade, hazel eyes, and glasses.

Ray leans over to speak to him. "You don't really do parties, do you?"

"No," he replies lethargically. "This is my brother's party; I didn't want to come, but our mom made me. Something about getting out and reconnecting with people, blah blah blah," he says sarcastically. "I'm Vincent, by the way."

"Good to meet you, Vincent, I'm Ray ... wait, didn't I see you earlier today?"

Vincent replies with a slight smile, "Yeah, you helped me earlier with those guys who were messing with me at the store, thanks."

"It's no problem, man, I—"

Before Ray could finish, Qasim comes running in from the entrance of the house, clearly intoxicated.

"Ray!" screams an inebriated Qasim. "Aye, bruh, you gotta go with me to meet Zeke and Trelle, bro!"

Ray tries to interject. "Oh, whoa, OK, man, I'm comin'! Nice meeting you, Vincent!" He manages a hurried goodbye as Qasim, in a drunken state, pulls him away. Vincent waves back, a sense of solitude creeping onto his face as he sinks back into his seat, left with a somewhat dejected expression.

* * *

Meanwhile, at the fringe of Piedmont Park, Jonathan Caine materializes abruptly, his arrival marked by a searing blaze of hellfire that scalds the ground beneath him, leaving a smoldering imprint.

"Well, well, here we are again." He drives his hands into the ground and surges a dark, powerful energy into the earth beneath him. He then begins to chant:

"Enter through the narrow gate"—the pulsing grows stronger—"for the gate is wide and the way is broad that leads to destruction"— the energy grows in power and the rubble starts to levitate—"and there are MANY who enter through it."

A sinister smirk stretches across his face, casting an eerie shadow over the vicinity. A sudden silence descends, nature itself hushing in eerie unison—crickets cease their chirping, owls stifle their calls, and the wildlife scatters in a panicked frenzy.

The ground quivers as the earth convulses, and from its depths, creatures draped in black and red hues burst forth. Their arrival reeks of despair and sulfur, eclipsing the natural scent of grass. The demons, emitting shrill, dissonant screeches, exhibit erratic movements—crawling, flying, and stalking, all converging toward Caine, aligning before him like a disciplined army facing their commander.

Caine's voice reverberates through the park, a chilling command carrying through the air. "We all have a role to play ... seek out the vulnerable, the easily swayed, and infuse their souls with darkness and agony. Hunt the pure-hearted and claim their essence for yourselves!" His fist tightens with determination. "We must channel every ounce of malevolent energy into the depths of hell, and when the time is ripe, we shall obliterate our foes and establish our supremacy forever!"

His words stir the demons into an ecstatic frenzy, fueling their mischief with passion. In an instant, they vanish into the city, eager to sow chaos and disorder, carrying out their master's nefarious scheme. Meanwhile, Caine assumes human form—a devilishly handsome man, tall, mid-forties, clad in a business suit. As he pounds the ground, a seismic disturbance harbingers the release of the demonic horde, creating an otherworldly earthquake.

With a calculated gaze fixed on the cityscape, he summons a portal of darkness, casting one final glance before disappearing into its mysterious depths.

* * *

Back at the party, Qasim introduces Ray to Trelle and Zeke. Dontrelle is really the only one paying attention and talking to Ray and Qasim about social issues. Ezekiel has his eyes set on Viera, while another woman is trying to get Ezekiel's attention.

"Damn yo! Yeen gotta act like that, aight!" Zeke says as he lets her go. She snatches her hand and she and Khalia leave the house in a hurry.

"Aight, everything's good," says a young fraternity member. "Everybody can go home, thank you for coming out! Please exit through the front!"

As people begin to leave, Zeke grabs one of the girls who seems to still be shaken up. He asks her to stay and let him console her. She agrees and he walks her to his room. Dontrelle shakes his head and puts his hand to his forehead after watching what transpired. Qasim grabs Dontrelle by the shoulder.

"Aye, man, let him have his fun, as long as she consents," relays Qasim coming back to his senses from his own drunken stupor.

"Y'know I just wish he'd have a better head on his shoulders instead of an ... ass," replies Dontrelle. Qasim laughs in response and notices Ray out of the corner of his eye.

Ray is staring off into space and thinking to himself. Why didn't I feel it? he thought. Everyone else felt it, why didn't I? In the moment that the quake happened, Ray honestly didn't feel it. He saw everyone's reaction and just followed suit to not stand out. When everyone else felt the quake, it was as if nothing happened to him. He stood there in a daze, confused and somewhat frightened.

"Ray!" exclaims Qasim snapping Ray out of his trance and turning his attention to Qasim.

"Huh?!" questions Ray coming back to reality. "You should go home and check on Wott and make sure he's OK," says Qasim. "I know he's on your mind."

"Oh ... yeah, man, I should go but knowing him he slept through all of it," Ray says staring off awkwardly. He and Qasim dap up as usual. Ray also tells Dontrelle that it was great meeting him and shakes his hand as well. He leaves the home in a blur, walks to his car, gets in it and sits for a moment. Something's just not right, he thinks to himself.

On his way home, he ponders if something happened to him in the past few days. He retraces every moment he can think of in the last seventy-two hours, but cannot come to a conclusion. He soon arrives at home. He gets out of the car, locks it behind him, walks toward

45

the door and unlocks it. He walks in. Nothing is damaged or moved.

He walks to his room to check on his faithful canine companion. And Wott is sitting in his dog bed, sound asleep. He tiptoes to his bedroom where he undresses, takes a shower, sets his alarm clock and gets into bed. He ponders for a moment. Maybe it's all just a coincidence. Hopefully, everything will be fine by tomorrow. He closes his eyes and begins to dream.

Chapter 5: Celestial Revelations

In a realm devoid of both darkness and light, God manifests on one side, and the Devil appears on the other. They engage in conversation.

"You seem to have forced my hand," God remarks.

The Devil retorts, "The last champion of light you selected made our task so much easier. I hope that legacy continues."

"This one might pose a challenge for your agent," God states.

"He has yet to fail me. He will triumph over your team of elemental warriors once more," the Devil asserts. "With any luck, this one will possess the same tenacity as the last."

In this cosmic confrontation, both God and the Devil exchange words, their rivalry eternally entwined.

God's voice resonates with unwavering determination. "The balance must be upheld. Their free will is the essence of this conflict."

The Devil smirks, shrouded in darkness. "Free will, a beautiful illusion. Our struggle persists, regardless."

"Yet hope persists within them," God counters, radiating an aura of boundless faith.

"Hope, a fleeting ember in the face of temptation," the Devil chuckles darkly. "It fuels our eternal dance."

Their discourse, an endless dialogue between opposing forces, shapes the fate of realms unknown. The battle of light and darkness, waged through champions and agents, ripples across existence, each encounter a testament to the cosmic struggle for the souls of mortals.

Meanwhile, the items in Ray's room are wrapped in a thin layer of white light and float slightly in the air. Ray awakens and it causes everything to drop just before he rises to see everything fall but notices the shaking of everything.

"Was that an aftershock?!" says Ray, attributing the shaking of things to last night's earthquake. With a swift motion, he snatches his phone from the nightstand, bounding out of bed. He then opens social media and the local news pages. There was nothing about aftershocks online. He shakes his head. "And it continues," he says, throwing his phone across the bed and turns his back to go shower. Yet, it doesn't land there; it floats midair, enveloped in a strange light.

"Damn, I forgot my towels," he mutters walking back out of the bathroom and into the closet. He walks into the closet but notices the phone floating and walks out backward slowly and stares intently.

"I'm dreaming, I'm dreaming, I'm dreaming ...," he says repeatedly.

He slowly walks toward the bed with a feeling of fear. He reaches out and his hand begins to glow bright white. He begins to breathe hard with a look of confusion and concern on his face. He tenses his hand and the phone begins to float toward him. The look of concern soon turns to a look of wonder. The phone slowly but surely comes to him and he grasps it and the light disappears. "What? ...," he utters with a quiet tone. He examines the room and ponders what else he could pull toward him.

In his curiosity, he looks at his deodorant stick. He extends his hand out and then hesitates. "Wait a minute," he thinks out loud. Stepping back, creating distance, he aims to truly test this inexplicable power within him. He reaches out his hand and tenses it slightly and the mysterious light energy surrounds the deodorant stick. He increases the tension and it picks up speed, moving closer to him. He then thinks that he wants it now and in an instant, it flies into his hands.

"Bruh, huh huh huh! Oh my God!" he says in an electrifying rush of excitement, astonishment written across his face.

Soon, he's walking around the house grabbing different objects, pulling them around and placing them in new spots. "This is unreal!" he screams with excitement. His dog wakes up, looks up and tries to ignore what he sees in favor of his morning sleep.

"I wonder what else I can do?" questions Ray looking at his palms with a smile.

"You will know, in due time ...," echoes a disembodied voice.

Ray's curiosity and fun soon turns to fear and worry. He thought an intruder had entered his house but unbeknownst to him it had entered his mind. "Whoa wait, who is that, where are you?!" Ray asks with a look of confusion on his face. He saw no one but heard them clearly. He examines the room and looks at his dog. "Can I communicate with animals or something?" He leans into his dog. "Wott ... can you speak?" he questions.

Wott barks.

"Oh, OK," he says with disappointment, standing and walking back toward his room.

"You must find others, like you," relays the voice.

Ray stops in his tracks and questions the voice. "Who are they?" asks Ray, confused about where the voice is coming from while trying to cling to sanity. "Where do I find them?"

The voice replies, "You already have the answers," in a fortified tone. "Now, go and find the others."

Ray's face becomes a canvas of mixed emotions. Wonder, fear, confusion, and excitement sweep over him, painting his expression and demeanor with a myriad of feelings. His curiosity eclipses all other senses, driving him to stare at the floor for a brief moment before darting off to his room. There, he swiftly takes a shower, tends to his grooming, selects his attire, and with a determined look and intense gaze, strides toward the door. He jumps into his truck, revs the engine, and speeds off into the heart of the city, heading straight for Zeke and Trelle's house in pursuit of more answers.

* * *

Meanwhile, as the dawn breaks, Viera awakens in Khalia's room, her thoughts consumed by the events of the previous night. Upon arriving home, she found her sisters unharmed, but her mother, back from a gambling spree, was inebriated. In a drunken tirade, her mother dismissed the sitter, accusing Viera of irresponsibility and neglect toward her sisters for leaving them during the earthquake. Despite her mother's harsh words, Viera understood that it was fueled by frustration and intoxication. Fortunately, Khalia intervened, waiting for Viera's response and offering her a place to stay the night, diffusing the tense situation.

While Khalia continues to sleep, Viera hops out of bed and notices that the lights are on and that the wind chimes near the windows in Khalia's room are clanging. She feels a slight breeze around her neck but the windows are closed. She walks over to the chimes and stops them. As she turns to walk away, they begin to move again. She turns around with a confused look and tries to rationalize the phenomenon.

"She stay makin' somethin'," she says to herself, attributing Khalia's passion for technology to the creation of the automated windchimes. She walks to the bathroom and opens her overnight bag that sits on Khalia's large vanity.

Viera reaches in her toiletry bag to pull out her toothbrush and fumbles it, as it falls to the ground. She reaches out her hand and a strange gust of air throws the toothbrush toward the ceiling. Viera gasps, stands back and looks at her hand. Viera's voice sliced through the tension, laden with a mix of disbelief and gripping fear.

"What the hell was that?" Her words quiver, edged with an undeniable sense of dread that resonates in the air, her eyes wide with alarm. She motions her hand and it seems to not happen for a second time. She looks at her hands. "I have to be going crazy ..." She slowly picks up the toothbrush and looks at it, grips it with the palm of her hand and closes her eyes, then breathes and relaxes her grip.

She slowly widens her eyes and sees the toothbrush standing up in her palm and it's surrounded by a small whirlwind, her hair is flickering with a smooth breeze caressing it and soon the items in the bathroom are floating: The towels, Khalia's makeup, her toiletry bag and its contents are swirling around her and a fear overcomes her and all the items drop. She screams and Khalia wakes up out of the bed in a fluster as she runs to the bathroom.

"V! What's wrong, are you OK?!" yells Khalia as she enters the bathroom. Khalia looks around at all the items on the bathroom floor. "Girl, what's going on? What happened?" questions Khalia in confusion about the messy state her bathroom is in.

"Girl, I, I, I don't know, something ... something's not right. Your wind chimes and the toothbrush ...," stutters a distraught Viera.

"Girl, calm down, it's OK," she says. Khalia grabs Viera by the arms and Viera screams again.

"Ouch, girl, you shocked me!" exclaims Viera.

"Oh damn, girl, I'm sorry!" relays Khalia apologizing.

"Oh my God ... Lia .... look at your fingertips ...," says Viera in shock at the sight in front of them both.

Khalia looks down at her hands. There's electricity zipping across her hands, dancing from finger to finger, causing a flickering light to dance across her face while Viera looks on with concern and fear. Khalia begins to smile and focuses her attention on the lights in the bathroom.

"Khalia ... no ...," says a concerned Viera immediately grasping what her best friend is thinking.

"What, girl?!" Khalia says in a defensive tone. "I'm not gonna do anything!"

"Uh huh ...," says Viera folding her arms and judging her best friend. Khalia immediately zaps the electricity from her fingertips toward the vanity lights in her bathroom; it causes a massive power surge, the lights in the house flicker and showers the bathroom with electricity. In the calamity, Viera ducked to avoid the spark. She slowly rises and addresses Khalia. "Girl .... just ... why?"

Khalia interrupts for an exposition. "OK, V, something amazing has happened and we can't ignore it."

"Girls! You OK up there?!" questions Khalia's mom trying to assess the situation with the power surge unbeknownst to her that her daughter has caused it.

"Yeah, Mama, we're good!" exclaims Khalia to affirm that she and Viera are "fine." "OK, something happened to us last night, I don't know what but, it's really—"

Viera interrupts in a fearful tone, "Scary AF, uh yeah!"

"No this is, this is a change ...," replies a content Khalia who smiles at the revelation. "This is exactly the change I've been looking for in my life."

"Uh-uh, I don't need no kinda changes right now!" exclaims Viera completely in opposition to the power she has witnessed from both her and her friend. "OK, we need to figure this out, what happened last night?!"

Both girls stop to think. Khalia makes an observation. "The earthquake, it must have caused some sort of supernatural phenomenon and that caused everyone to get superpowers!" Khalia continues, "You think our parents got 'em too?!"

"I pray to the good Lord that my mama doesn't have superpowers ...," says Viera sarcastically as she flips her hands back and forth, staring at them waiting for something to happen. She clenches her palm and motions her hand in a back-handed wave and a gust of air closes, slams the door shut and knocks Khalia back.

"Woo!" exclaims Khalia as she falls down. "Oh my God! Girl, I'm so sorry!" exclaims Viera concerned about Khalia's well-being.

Khalia laughs while standing. "OK that was payback for shocking you. Look let's get dressed and go figure this out, we gotta get some answers," says Khalia getting up off the floor and running to the guest bathroom to shower.

Viera stands in the bathroom and stares off into space. She's in complete disbelief at what just happened this morning. She'd become a superhero in a matter of minutes. She begins to worry about her mom and her sisters. What if they had powers too? What if ...

"Viera! Stop thinking and get in the shower!" screams Khalia from the guest bathroom.

Viera breaks her thought process saying, "Aight, girl! OK!" as Viera scrambles to get ready. Both girls take showers and scurry to get dressed. They both grab their things and run downstairs.

"OK, let's retrace our steps from last night," whispers Khalia.

"Girls, what was all the commotion upstairs?" questions Khalia's mom.

"Oh we just freaked out from the lights flashing, Mama," replies a lying Khalia. "Hey, Mrs. Brown, could you do somethin' for me?" Viera pauses, her tone gentle yet insistent. "Could you hold out your arm for a minute?"

"Um, Alright, Viera ...," says a confused Mrs. Brown.

"Now hold out your hand, palm forward and clench it," says Viera. Both girls stand in the kitchen and brace for something to happen, but nothing does, they continue to look at Mrs. Brown with concerned looks on their faces.

"Girls, what's happening here?" Khalia's mom queries, her posture stiff and oddly posed, a perplexed expression etched upon her face.

Thinking quick on her feet Khalia replies, "Yea! That's it, Ma! That's the ... the ... that's the grip! Yeaaaaa that's the grip!"

"Well, it needs a little something extra, it's way too plain," she replies. "Somethin' like this!" Khalia's mom begins doing a dip in the middle of the kitchen and the girls start to chuckle.

"See now this is what I'm talking 'bout!" exclaims Khalia's mom.

The girls start backing out of the kitchen toward the door and Khalia grabs her keys. "OK, Mama, you keep getting it in and we're gonna head on out," quips Khalia.

"OK, girls! Be careful!" replies her mother continuing to dance.

"We will," reply the girls in unison, opening the door and exiting.

Khalia closes the door behind her. "OK, let's go," replies an enthusiastic Khalia.

They hop in Khalia's Range Rover.

"OK where should we go first?" asks Viera. Khalia puts her foot on the brake and pushes the button to start her car.

"I think we have to go back to Trelle and Zeke's place," replies Khalia. She puts her foot to the gas, leaves the driveway and turns onto the street.

"Ugh, do we really have to go there?" asks an annoyed Viera.

"Unfortunately, yeah," replies Khalia. "That's where we were when the quake happened, so that's really where we need to start."

"Y'know it could have been that waffle house we visited before we went to your house," interjects Viera.

Khalia stops at a red light and stares at Viera for a moment. "OK, girl, damn," replies Viera. The light turns green and Khalia drives toward Ezekiel and Dontrelle's townhouse.

* * *

Meanwhile, Ray pulls up to Dontrelle and Ezekiel's townhome. He gets out of the truck and looks around searching for anything that may be a clue to the recent change in his life. The events from last night start to play through his head. The earthquake must've caused him and the people at the party to get powers, but he couldn't have gotten powers because he couldn't even feel the quake. He felt like Static Shock after the Bang Baby incident. He walks up toward the house and heads for the front door. His focus is cut short, he feels a tremor of the earth and stops in his tracks.

"Whoa, was that another quake?" questions Ray as he braces himself. The tremor stops. Ray looks on in confusion. The ground moves again with another tremor that lasts only for a moment. "What the hell is going on?" questions Ray baffled by the current situation.

He looks around and sees two pitch-black humanoid figures behind Dontrelle and Ezekiel's home; he stares at them, and they notice Ray is watching them. In an instant, they vanish.

OK, what's next? thinks Ray. Suddenly he hears someone yell and then sees Dontrelle fly out of the trees riding a boulder and heads straight for Ray! "AYE!" screams Ray as he dodges a floating Dontrelle. Dontrelle loses his train of thought and gets sent flying toward the ground and crashes.

"Ahh, c'mon, Trelle, gotta do better than that!" exclaims Zeke emerging from the trees with a fireball on the tip of his extended index and middle finger. Ray looks at him with a shocked look on his face.

"Aye yo, you Qasim's homeboy from the party last night, uhh ..." Zeke's voice trails off as he struggles to recall the name. Dontrelle gets back on his feet, dusts himself off and jogs toward the two.

"Aye, Ray, right?" asks Dontrelle, easily remembering Ray's name. "What's up? What you doing here?"

"Well ... something told me to come back here and well," says Ray as his thoughts trail off as he looks off again into the wooded area. They both look at him with a bewildered look.

"Aye, you had some bad bud last night or something?" asks Zeke attributing Ray's despondence to a bad marijuana trip.

"OK, you can control fire and you can control ground I guess?" asks Ray his gaze shifting between the abilities of the two. With a subtle focus, Ray utilizes his powers, lifting the boulder that Dontrelle previously rode upon. Lowering it gently, he redirects his attention to Dontrelle and Zeke. "So trust me, if I'm feeling weird things, I think that's the least of my worries at the moment," replies Ray, a hint of urgency tainting his voice.

While the guys are talking, Khalia and Viera pull up in Khalia's car and get out. "So I'm guessing we're just in time for the next party?" quips Khalia looking around and then affixing her gaze upon the group.

"I'm guessing you two came for some answers too?" asks Ray recognizing the two from the party last night.

"Yeah, but it might not be the answer we want," replies a concerned Viera. "Hey, mean girl," Zeke says sarcastically.

"Hey, assho—"

Khalia interrupts Viera. "V!"

"What?!" replies Viera glaring at Zeke with major disdain.

"He really ain't worth it and he has powers too; we gotta figure this stuff out together ... unfortunately," Khalia says making the connection that everyone in attendance has some type of power.

While the group is talking, the fire that Ezekiel was flinging around in the forest catches on to nearby trees and starts a blaze.

"Oh, whoa!" screams Ray as he attempts to protect everyone as a pseudo human shield.

"Zeke, put it out, man!" exclaims Dontrelle motioning Zeke to use his powers to fix the situation with urgency.

"Alright, alright, hold up." Zeke reaches out his hands to stop the fire but the blaze intensifies causing other trees and bushes to catch fire as well.

"Oh, damn!" yells Zeke as he jumps back, unable to control the blaze and a fear begins to rise in his being.

"V, try to blow it out!" screams Khalia afraid that the blaze will start to spread.

Viera tries to use her powers but she can't.

"The whole place is gonna go up in flames!" exclaims Trelle.

Just in that moment, Vincent walks up from behind the group and raises his hands. A geyser of water comes rushing from his hands and he sprays it over the lit areas and then retracts the excess water back to his hands where it disappears.

"Whoa!" says Ray as he walks toward Vincent. "That was amazing, how'd you know what to do?"

"I just think about it and it kinda happens," murmurs Vincent.

"Hey, you're Vincent, right?" asks Ray as Vincent nods his head. "You were at the party last night too!"

"Yeah, I—" Again before Vincent can speak he's interrupted, this time by Zeke using his fire powers and shooting into the forest.

"Zeke, what the fuck! He just put it out!" exclaims Khalia.

"Nah yo, something was in the bushes," says Zeke with his eyes affixed and motions in swing looking for a shadowy figure.

In that moment, a shadow-like figure jumps out of the bushes and into a thicket of trees. Zeke shoots fire at it, misses and begins chasing after it.

"Aye, yo!" Zeke screams out and goes running toward the entity.

"Yo bro, wait!" yells Trelle as he chases after Zeke.

Khalia sighs starting to pull Viera along. "C'mon, V!"

"Oh! No, ma'am! That's not ... Whoaaaaa! Lia!" Before she can even finish her sentence, Viera is pulled along with Khalia moving at top speed.

"C'mon we better play catch up," says Ray to Vincent and they follow the others, running in the same direction.

Khalia and Viera catch up to Dontrelle and Zeke while they stand in the middle of the trees and look around.

"I don't see it anymore!" exclaims Zeke walking into a clearing and upset that he missed attacking the figure.

"What was it?" asks Khalia inquisitive as ever.

"I don't know, but it looked like it was watching us and was about to attack," replies Zeke as he sat down on a stump.

"Well, whatever it was, it looks like it's gone," replies Khalia as she sits down next to Dontrelle.

"Lia, how were you moving so fast?!" questions an out-of-breath Viera with her hands on her knees.

"I really don't know, it might be like a side effect of my powers, maybe," replies Khalia. "I don't know, girl, all this is really weird and even though I usually would have an answer, I don't ..."

Ray and Vincent catch up to them and stand around.

"Welcome to Superhero's 101, y'all take a seat," says a sarcastic Ezekiel acting like an instructor in a class.

"Nowhere to really sit," says Ray looking around for a seat.

"Hold on, I got you," replies Dontrelle motioning his hand to a nearby tree and uproots it and slowly brings it closer to the group.

"OK, so we know who's the strongest," replies Ray pointing out the power of Dontrelle's strength.

"Yeah, me," Khalia and Zeke reply simultaneously. They give each other a long, cold stare and then both chuckle. Viera turns her head and stares with concern.

"Well, look, something weird is going on in Atlanta," replies Ray. "Earthquakes, Black people with superpowers, weird shadowy things that are running around spying on people," he continues, seated on the tree Dontrelle lowered. "I mean, I don't know what's going on, but seeing as though we're the only ones with powers, we should stick together, ya know, get to know each other."

"Well, I'm Viera, I go to Spelman and I'm a Pisces," rebuts Viera.

"OK that's cool. Yeah why don't we all do that, ya name and something about you."

"Well, aight, I'm Dontrelle, y'all can call me Trelle and I'm Zeke's homeboy," replies Trelle while he shakes hands with Zeke.

"Well, I'm Khalia, you can't call me Lia, that's reserved for V," replies Khalia as they high-five.

"I'm Zeke, Zeke the freak, smooth as silk and hot like fire," says Zeke as he tries to spark a fire and fails. Everyone laughs and he smirks.

"I'm Ray, I'm from Alabama and I just work in IT," announces Ray while looking toward Vincent.

"What about you, Vincent? Tell us something," ponders Khalia.

"Well, um I'm Vincent and—," Vincent begins, but before he can finish, Ezekiel interrupts with a harsh personality.

"He a faggot," interrupts Zeke with a harsh tone and loud demeanor.

69

Viera, Khalia, and Ray look at Zeke with confusion. Dontrelle hangs his head down and speaks up.

"Come on, man, you don't have to be like that," says Trelle trying to get Zeke to stop his bigoted words. Vincent shuts down and looks at the ground, away from the group.

"What did you just say?" Ray questions, rising from his seat and fixing his gaze on Zeke, prepared to defend Vincent.

"I said he just a faggot," Zeke boldly says again standing in his conviction.

"Wait, how do you know that?" asks Viera pondering how Ezekiel made the statement.

"He's my brother, that's how I know," replies Zeke folding his arms and wearing a disappointed expression.

"That's REALLY how you talk to your brother? That's a damn shame!" exclaims Khalia her own anger beginning to rise like the flames that were previously extinguished in the forest.

"Aye, I call him as I see him and that's what I see," says Ezekiel leaning back while taking on everyone's opinion like an onslaught against a one-man army.

Before Khalia can speak, Ray intervenes. "Don't ever let me hear that, come out of your mouth again," firmly proclaims Ray extremely upset and pointing at Ezekiel.

"Look, don't get mad at me, get mad at the Bible, God himself said he don't like 'em," replies Zeke using a reference to back his own obtuse stance.

"The Bible also says that you shouldn't be having sex before marriage and judging by the girl you brought up to your room last night, your brother is no bigger a 'sinner' than you are," quips Ray.

As Ray and Zeke continue their argument, the shadows in the woods surrounding them begin moving around. "Y'all ...," says Viera shakily as she notices the change in the air. Ray and Zeke continue to argue. Viera nudges Khalia and Dontrelle and points out the shadows circling them. Dontrelle intervenes and stops their arguing and calls their attention to the shadows on the ground.

"Oh damn," whispers Zeke as beads of sweat begin to form on his forehead and his eyes widen.

The shadows surrounding them start taking form.

"Everybody, stay as calm as you can. Form a circle, back to back, Avengers style. Stand your ground," Ray commands, observing the shadows taking shape. The group follows his lead, assuming fighting stances. Ray slowly realizes they are transforming into the creatures from his dream two nights ago.

Hideous claws, snarling mouths, with horns atop their head and razor-sharp teeth, some with differing facial expressions and body compositions. Some seem stronger than others and hold different stances. "Listen on the count of three, if you can use your power to fight back, if you can't, fall back to the inside of the circle, alright?" states a tense yet prepared Ray.

Everyone agrees with a nod of approval.

"One ...," says Ray. A beast snarls in response. Fear begins to build among everyone, yet somehow they feel a sense of knowing what to do. "Two ...," Ray continues. The group tenses their hands, Khalia's lightning flickering across her fingertips, Dontrelle focusing on a nearby boulder, Viera causing the air to swirl around them. Vincent attempts to conjure water, but it's weaker than before. Ray notices his terror.

"Three!" Ray commands, forcefully pushing Vincent into the circle to seal the gap. Viera harnesses her powers, creating distance between the team and the encroaching creatures. Chaos erupts as the group desperately fends off the malevolent monsters charging toward them. Dontrelle, Khalia, Viera, and Ray exert themselves, striving to repel the advancing forces. Meanwhile, Ezekiel grapples with maintaining his flames, encountering difficulty in keeping them blazing.

"Zeke, what's going on, dude?!" asks Ray noticing that Zeke's fire power isn't working at the moment.

"Aye, man, I'm new to this, just like you don't ask me!" exclaims Zeke getting frustrated at Ray pointing out his current conundrum,

"Get inside with Vince, we'll cover you!" replies Ray.

Those words stir an uneasy emotion within Zeke. "I ain't no bitch like my BROTHER!"

Zeke yells as he charges the flames in his hands, aims them at the creatures and runs around the group knocking them all back but setting ablaze the forestry surrounding them and creating a blaze that surrounds the group.

"Zeke?!" screams a panicked Viera.

"Zeke, put it out!" yells Dontrelle trying to use his powers to smite the flames.

"I can't, man, I can't control it!" exclaims Zeke. The fire grows around them in a frenzy and the team huddles back-to-back together. Viera, Dontrelle and Ray continue to try using their powers to find a way out, but the flames become too large to move or put out!

"What do we do?!" screams Khalia, her panic taking over her being. Suddenly a large body of water appears over the group; it continuously expands and circulates and suddenly drops over the entire engulfed area and the team.

"Sorry ...," nervously states Vincent, lowering his hands.

"Well, ya know, the anticipation was great ...," replies Ray. "Let's just work on your execution a little bit more," he rebuts as he spits out a little water. They start to walk away from the charred bodies. Just as the steam settles, the creatures begin to rise and focus toward the group again.

"Wait what's going on?!" asks a startled Viera. "I thought Zeke burned them all!"

"Maybe they didn't burn all the way through," replies an anxious Dontrelle.

"What do we do?!" questions Ezekiel looking around for his next move. Ray closes his eyes and attempts to focus all of his energy into one huge blast but suddenly, a large beam of light envelops the area and the creatures surrounding them screech in agony and turn to dust in an instant. Behind the strong beam of light is a vague figure that stands before the group, the light in an instant dissipates with flickering twilights in its trace.

The team collectively stares at the man with each of them speaking of his familiar resemblance. "Hey ... I know you!" states Ray recalling the man from the day before.

"You were in the grocery store the other day!"

"Wait, no, I saw him outside my house the other day, he's a stalker!" interrupts an angry Viera.

"He was outside my home yesterday!" says Khalia also recalling her memory.

"I am sorry to interrupt your collective revelations," interrupts the man, "but if we do not move quickly more demons will come to attack."

"Demons? Like from hell, demons?!" asks Dontrelle with grave concern.

The man puts two fingers together and draws a line in the air with light energy from his fingertips and a portal opens. Ray's eyes widen. "Please, follow me, I will tell you much more once we are away from this area."

The man disappears into the portal. The group stands together in awe, collectively looking at each other with wonder, worry and bewilderment on their faces.

Ray steps toward the portal and stands in front of it. He reaches his hand in and snatches it back quickly from fear. He grabs his wrist, feels his hand and turns to the rest of the group. "C'mon, before more of those things start rollin' up on us." Ray walks through the portal and is enveloped by the light.

The others begin to walk toward the portal, but Ezekiel is apprehensive. "Aye yo, y'all gonna follow him, we don't know where that thing goes?!"

"Look, that guy knows somethin' and we need to figure it out together," says Khalia pointing out that he too has powers and motioning for Zeke to follow.

"Zeke, c'mon, man," says Dontrelle placing his hand on Zeke.

"Naw, man, I'm good. I'll deal with the demons or monsters or what the hell ever my damn self," replies Ezekiel with a sure disposition.

"Aight y'all let's go," replies Viera standing next to the portal being the last one to walk toward it.

The group one by one walks into the portal while Ezekiel stays behind. In that moment, a larger demon walks out of the forest with a horde of demons behind him. Zeke's adrenaline begins to pump and beads of sweat begin to form on his forehead.

"I got this, I got this," he repeats to himself. He starts up the fire in his hands and shoots it at the larger demon and it doesn't even faze him. Zeke begins to have second thoughts. His eyes widen and the flames in his hands begin to fade. "Naw, never mind!" exclaims Zeke as he runs toward the portal and jumps in moments before the horde of demons grabs him.

Chapter 6: Elemental Beginnings

Ezekiel falls in front of the group after jumping through the portal. Dontrelle and Vincent help him up onto his feet and he snatches his arm away from Vincent. "I'm good," he says as he looks around with the rest of the group.

The group finds themselves within what appears to be a base of operations, enclosed by walls of cold, unyielding steel. On these metallic surfaces, an array of screens depicting different corners of the globe hang, each pulsating with real-time data and images. These displays weave a tapestry of the world's activities, providing a mysterious backdrop to the unknown area enclosing the group.

At the opposite end of this expansive room, three colossal monitors stand sentinel, their screens flickering with a cascade of intricate data. A keyboard sits poised in front of these towering screens, surrounded by an array of chairs suggesting a place for strategizing or analysis. Khalia, overcome with awe, wanders the technologically advanced expanse, mesmerized by the sophistication woven into every corner of the space. "Where are we and when can I move in?" she exclaims.

"This place will serve as your base of operations," says the man emerging from the shadows of the room. "I am Kilik Hue." Kilik Hue stands at five foot nine, has beige skin, and looks wise beyond his years.

"Great to meet you, now you think you can tell us exactly what the hell is happening here?" quips Viera. "We all have these powers and—" Viera is interrupted.

"Ah, yes, your powers," acknowledges Hue. "Your abilities should be nearing battle readiness. You all managed to hold your ground against the demons before I arrived, especially you, Water," Hue remarks, pointing toward Vincent. He smiles and moves toward the room's center, the group instinctively gravitates along.

"You six have been selected as the next warriors in the eternal fight for balance," Hue elaborates with a smile. "Chosen to be the Elementals."

"Elementals?" questions Dontrelle raising a brow and tilting his head.

"Yes, six warriors divinely chosen to lead the charge against the Devil and his malevolent forces."

"Wai-wait, wait, what?" stutters Viera, grappling to comprehend her sudden induction into this new reality. Master Hue's fingers touch the screen of the central computer, initiating the unfolding of an ancient narrative.

"Thousands of years ago, God and the Devil struck an accord in anticipation of Armageddon. God, seeing the necessity for a balance between light and darkness, devised this pact to avert a conflict capable of triggering another cosmic reset—the collision of their powers potent enough to birth a new universe, ushering in a cycle of evolution afresh. Essential to this pact was a solemn oath: Neither deity would tread upon Earth. They vowed to uphold a balance, exerting influence upon the inhabitants of this realm. But the Devil, as ever, harbored divergent intentions.

"Following the pact's creation, the Devil fashioned a demon of unparalleled might and malevolence—Jonathan Caine. His mission on Earth encompassed two objectives: amassing souls to reinforce the demonic ranks and tipping the scales in favor of darkness. In response to this sinister initiative, God handpicked six individuals to lead the charge against Caine, endowing them with mastery over the most potent energies of heaven and earth—the Elements.

"Air, Lightning, Water, Fire, Earth, and Light. The inaugural team engaged Caine in combat, restoring equilibrium to Earth. Alas, despite the elemental power wielded against him, Caine's might proved impervious to destruction. It merely subdued him for approximately five hundred years. A new team is anointed every five centuries, heralding the resurgence of the battle."

"So ... we're the new team and it's our job to stop some super powerful demon and restore balance to the world?" Dontrelle inquires.

"Yes, moreover, as none of you were warriors or soldiers before today, you've been bestowed with the residual muscle memory of the preceding Elemental warriors. Over time, you'll refine this legacy, honing and crafting your individual fighting styles—forging them into your own."

"Wait, in time?" questions Khalia concerned about the latter statement from Hue.

"If Caine is already here, then shouldn't we be out fighting now?"

"You're still in the process of mastering your powers and learning to combat the demons," Hue responds walking stoically. "Simultaneously, the demons under Caine's command require sustenance from negative human energy to reach their full strength on Earth. Thus, they too need time to amass their energies."

"Wait, so how do we 'beat him,' Caine?" questions Trelle placing his hand on his chin.

Master Hue strides toward a concealed wall, his hand deftly finding a hidden switch that unveils a magnificent golden crown adorned with encased thorns and striking turquoise accents. "Behold the Crown of Thorns, an exceedingly rare relic crafted in the twelfth century. Fashioned from blessed gold, legend has it that it holds the power to obliterate any demonic energy it encounters, in the right hands," clarifies Hue.

"And here's where your role emerges, Ray. You harness the element of light, much like I do. As your direct predecessor, I'll personally mentor you, refining your powers and preparing you for a head-on confrontation with Caine." Hue's voice resonates with unwavering determination.

"Wait, don't we ALL need training?!" exclaims a questioning Ezekiel, his body language expressing his discontent.

"Yeah, I don't think any of us are okay with ONLY having muscle memory to rely on," replies Viera rolling her eyes and folding her arms to her body.

"Yes, I'll be overseeing your training as well. However, in Ray's case, training will become a constant endeavor, his primary occupation. So while the rest of you continue with your regular daily routines—," clarifies Master Hue.

"Wait, hold on," Ray interjects, his voice riddled with confusion and disbelief. "As much as being a superhero is literally all I ever wanted to be since I was a kid, I have a job. A home to pay for, student loans, and a dog to take care of. As much as I want to, I can't just drop everything to become a ... God warrior?!" His dismay is palpable in his words.

"I've accounted for all of these matters and made provisions," replies Hue calmly. "Your loans, credit cards, and mortgage have all been settled, and a substantial amount of funds has been deposited into your account, enough to cover your expenses for the next one to five years."

Ray's expression shifts to sheer bewilderment. "If you don't believe me, check your accounts." He hurriedly opens his phone to his banking apps, where he discovers his mortgage, car loan, and student loans all marked as paid, accompanied by a staggering $500,000 deposited into his savings account. Stunned, he stands there in disbelief.

"Wait, do we get that as well?" asks Dontrelle with a yearning in his eyes.

"I've covered some of your expenses, but not everyone received the same provisions as Ray," Hue explains, his expression reflecting a sense of resigned equity.

"Why the hell not?!" Zeke's voice echoes, infused with a stronger discontent than before. The rest of the team joins Ezekiel, standing united in their questioning.

"Ray is the light and thus the leader of this team," Hue explains. "His power surpasses that of all of you combined." His voice holds an unwavering certainty. "In due time, he'll perform feats that surpass imagination. Light energy is the bane of darkness; it means Ray will face Caine head-on. His task is to defeat Caine and preserve the balance. The team's role is to support him."

"Feels like we're Ray and the Rayettes," Viera quips, a touch of dejection in her voice as she glances down. The rest of the team mirrors her sentiments, all wrestling with a shared thought: "What's the use of my power when Ray's power overshadows everything?"

Ray glances away, his expression uncertain, before lifting his gaze to address the team. "Hey, I know it sounds like I'm supposed to be the 'lead,' but I want us all to work as a team. We're all just as important as the other. Otherwise, I would be the only one with powers." The others exchange glances and nod in agreement, except for Ezekiel, who keeps his gaze fixed elsewhere, wearing an irritated expression.

Ray notices but does not address it as not to draw from the current matter at hand. "OK so, when do we start training?" he questions walking toward Master Hue and looking at the huge screens.

"Do we need to bring a change of clothes?" asks Khalia pondering if there are uniforms involved.

"Let me get your combat uniforms; they'll double as your training gear." Master Hue heads toward the opposite side of the base, prompting the team to start exploring the area.

"Y'all look at this." Khalia scurries to the computer area. "This system is crazy, and its monitoring capabilities are amazing," expresses Khalia. "You can not only observe all of Georgia and the States but all over the world!"

"Yes, the system was set up to monitor the entire world for demonic activity, when something happens you will be able to know immediately," replies Hue, bringing in the old uniforms from the last team.

"Oh wow, these are old ...," replies Viera picking up the sleeves of the ancient attire with disdain sprawled across her face.

"Yes, the previous team and I would wear these when we would fight," Hue says recalling memories of his time as an Elemental.

"Khalia's face twists in confusion. "Hold up, when were these created?" she asks, puzzled. "Around 1520, why do you ask?" questions Master Hue.

"That would make you more than five hundred years old ...," replies Khalia questioning Hue's honesty.

"Yes I am 547 years old to be exact; temporary immortality tends to do that to you."

"OK, this armor ain't gonna cut it if we're supposed to be dodging and fighting. We need something more ... practical," Viera remarks. "I could whip up a design, but I could use a hand. Hey, Vincent, you down to lend me some help?"

Vincent had been keeping to himself, soaking in all the info flying around for the past hour. He grins and nods, eager to assist Viera.

Ray inspects the armor. "We need gear that's quick to throw on, yet tough enough to handle whatever's coming at us."

88

Khalia responds with a smiling chuckle, "I really hate how coincidental this is, but I took some software from my dad's lab the other day." She walks toward the base computers and pulls out a flash drive from her wallet. "It's a program that can instantaneously create matter when it's activated. Maybe I could create a program that creates our armor with some sort of activation action?" Khalia turns to address the group. "Does anyone know where I can get Kevlar?"

"Umm, Zeke and I know some frat in the police department who might be able to hook us up with some stuff," says Dontrelle remembering a fraternity brother who works on the police force.

"OK, get me as much as you can." Khalia cracks her knuckles and smiles. "Time to go to work."

As the rest of the team spends time preparing the new outfits for battle, Master Hue pulls Ray to the side before he speaks up. "Come with me." Master Hue leads Ray toward a door.

He opens the door and Ray follows behind. They exit to a lush opening to a forest where there is an open field and trees that billow in the air, a calm, serene area dedicated to focus and strength. "These are the training grounds, it is here where all teams have learned to use their powers and forged their fighting skills for combat." Master Hue reaches out his hand and a white bō staff flies from a weaponry stand from far away. "This was my previous weapon before I retired it. You may practice with it if you wish."

Ray takes the staff into his hand and examines it. He begins to twist and turn it. With the knowledge of using the staff flowing through his head he begins to adjust his stance and strike at the air while completing movements.

"Excellent! You're already experienced it seems," exclaims Hue noticing that Ray has already grasped weaponry.

"Not so much experience, so much as a lot of time watching anime and playing video games," quips Ray while walking toward Master Hue.

"Ray, I want you to understand, YOU must train until you have perfected your skills and powers. The others have a part to play as well, but you must become the lead of this team if you have any hope of stopping Caine. How far are you on controlling your light energy?"

90

Ray readjusts the staff in his hands and throws it like a spear toward a nearby cliff. He immediately points his finger toward the moving staff and uses his powers to stop it and then returns it back to himself.

"Impressive but needs improvement indeed." Master Hue levitates off the ground and begins to fly. Ray stands with his mouth agape. "Once you have mastered your light energy, the world will become your oyster," he continues, "only then ..." Master Hue builds light energy into his right hand like an orb and shoots it at a tree nearby, burning a hole straight through it causing it to fall. He then uses his light energy to catch the tree before it can fall and guides it gently to the ground. "...will you be able to truly lead this team." Hue walks toward Ray. "Are you ready to train?"

"Yes, but I want the rest of the team here too," replies Ray concerned that they should all be training.

"As you wish." Master Hue opens another portal and uses his light energy to bring the rest of the team to the practice field by cloaking them in the energy and forcing them to the training grounds.

"Whoa! Hey! Can you warn us the next time you decide to do that!" exclaims Khalia distraught with being forced away from her technological advancements.

"Where are we?" questions Viera standing up and taking in the area of the training grounds.

"Oh, these are the training grounds. Hue brought me here to show me this is where we're gonna be training," says Ray with an eager smile on his face.

Ezekiel hangs back, his observant eyes catching not only Master Hue showing Ray the training grounds without involving the rest of the team, but also the sight of a new white staff in Ray's hand.

"My apologies for the abrupt intrusion, where are we with the training attire?" questions Hue pondering how far Khalia had come in the last hour.

"I'm almost done with the program for materialization, we just need the materials and designs," Khalia responds sure of herself.

"Damn, girl, that was fast!" exclaims Viera surprised at Khalia's speed.

Khalia replies. "I can work pretty fast on something I really want."

"We can get the materials tomorrow," replies Dontrelle adding to the current conversation.

"And we can finish up the designs tomorrow," Vincent adds softly.

"Excellent, then let your team training commence ... now!" announces Master Hue, channeling elemental energy into his right hand, shaping a sphere, and propelling it toward Dontrelle. Khalia blinks and suddenly time seems to slow down around her. She witnesses the energy sphere hurtling toward Dontrelle at a reduced pace. Reacting swiftly, she dashes toward him, leaving traces of crackling lightning in her wake. Just moments before the energy sphere strikes, she reaches Dontrelle and moves him out of harm's way.

Everything snaps back to normal speed. Khalia has moved Dontrelle to the opposite side of the field, averting the blast's path, and now stands alongside him. They exchange a brief smile, then Hue breaks the silence.

"Excellent job, Lightning." Khalia stares at Hue. "From what I see all of your powers are beginning to advance rapidly. It is truly time for us all to begin now."

"Wait, in these clothes?" replies Viera concerned about her Louis Vuitton shoes.

Ray looks over to see Vincent standing away from everyone, looking at the sunset. Ray walks over. "Hey, Vincent, you OK?"

Vincent replies, "Hey, Ray, yeah I'm OK."

Ray responds, "Hey, about what your brother said back there, he shouldn't be saying that to you."

Vincent replies, "I mean it's not like it's not true ..."

Ray's face adjusts to one of sincerity. "Even if it is, you shouldn't let him talk about you like that, man. That's not all you are, OK?"

Vincent turns back to look at the sunset. "I don't know why I'm here, Ray, God is supposed to hate ... someone like me or someone who feels the way I feel."

Ray places his hand on Vincent's shoulder. "Vincent ... remember you're supposed to be here. You were chosen by God, handpicked to fight, you are meant to be here. He loves you and believes in you." Ray turns and points at the team. "We were chosen to do something amazing. That's what you should focus on, that's all you need to know."

Vincent smiles and speaks. "Thanks, Ray." They share a smile. Off in the background, Ezekiel watches them inquisitively.

Vincent and Ray walk back toward the group.

Master Hue says, "Ah, excellent, just in time." Master Hue uses his light energy to project an image. "We're going to talk about types of demons." Master Hue changes the light energy to project the first demons. The majority of which, the team faced earlier. "These are called Treks, they are your average attacking demon. Some of them can attack with great speed, you must be cautious; if one is on its hind legs, that is an indication that it's faster than its other counterparts."

The group looks on listening intently.

Master Hue alters his light energy and projects the next two demons. "These next two demons are the dwellers of land and sky, respectively." He continues, "Scrabblers and pinions. Scrabblers attack from below in a crawling fashion. Pinions attack from the sky, striking down on a foe." Master Hue changes his light energy for the last time. "And finally these are behemoths, powerful, large demons that can overpower you if they grapple you, you will need to use all your strength to break free."

Ezekiel turns toward Master Hue. "OK, so how do we use our powers to take them out?" He continues, "When we were fighting them in the park, they were wounded, but they didn't stay down?"

Master Hue explains, "Your powers are still in the process of development. To wield them effectively, you must refine your control by mastering your mindsets and emotions." With a commanding gesture, he opens a portal, revealing a demon from outside the pocket dimension of the training area. As it steps through, he promptly seals the portal shut. "Once you've gained mastery over your energies, most demons will become remarkably easier to overcome."

The behemoth strides forward, and Khalia unleashes her lightning upon it, leaving a noticeable impact but not enough to obliterate the creature. As it lunges toward her, she instinctively prepares for the imminent impact. In an instant, Hue unleashes an energy projectile, causing the behemoth to disintegrate.

"Like so ," states Master Hue, a pleased smile forming on his face.

Khalia's heart races in her chest, a mix of exhilaration and relief coursing through her. "Alright, let's begin!" she exclaims eagerly, brimming with enthusiasm.

Two days later ...

The team is down in the base of operations and Khalia is putting finishing touches on the program for the suits. "OK, almost done ... GOT IT!" She stands and takes a steel smart band off of the USB base. "OK so, who wants to test it out?"

Ray steps up. "I'll give it a shot!" Ezekiel scrunches his face to showcase his annoyance.

Khalia grabs Ray's wrist. "OK, I used nanobots to create a program that when we charge this band, with our pure elemental energy. Our armored suits will materialize on our bodies over our clothes. They're made using Viera's designs and use the various materials in the band to replicate and build upon themselves. They'll form a fit, so just do some shopping and adjust your wardrobe as needed and if you have on a coat, take it off first. Ray, are you ready to give it a try?"

Ray nods and Khalia and the team stand back. He charges the band with his light energy, slowly the energy envelopes his body. He observes and smiles. He is draped in the color-coded armor and a headband adorns his head. "LIT!" he exclaims. The team and Master Hue smile.

Khalia says, "Alright, everybody, suit up, time to train."

Chapter 7: Demon Time

As the evening descends upon Atlanta, a gentle breeze carries the autumn chill, enveloping the area in a serene aura. An elderly woman basks in the beauty of the sunset while nearby, two children play joyously. Leaves, kissed by the season's touch, cascade from the trees, adding to the tranquility. All seems peaceful until an abrupt disruption fractures the scene—a shift in energy that catches the attention of the nearby woman.

From the thicket of trees, Caine materializes, in his demon form. The woman, sensing the anomaly, discreetly averts her gaze, feigning indifference to avoid drawing attention. Caine's smirk grows sinister as he instantaneously reverts to his human guise; 6'4" muscular, white male with a bald head in a tailored suit. With a casual air, he approaches the woman, inquiring politely if the seat is taken before settling beside her.

Unaware of the horror she had glimpsed moments ago, the woman glances back in the direction of the terrifying creature, oblivious that the very entity now sits merely inches away from her.

"Such a lovely evening, isn't it?" Caine asks the elderly woman with a seemingly approachable demeanor. She fidgets around to see Caine smiling at her and then takes in the scenery before him. She relaxes and replies.

"Oh, yes ... indeed ... it is ... very lovely," she says nervously trying to break from her nervousness.

"Is something bothering you? Are you alright?" replies Caine in a calm tone.

"Oh, it's nothing." She chuckles easing her nerves. "Oh just this old mind playing tricks on me."

"Oh? Tell me what did it see?" He acts entirely oblivious to his own appearance.

"Oh I thought I saw a ..." She turns to him and sees his eyes are pitch-black. She gasps shakily and closes her eyes. "Oh God," she mutters under her breath and shudders in Caine's presence.

"Oh yes, him ... he has made some beautiful things hasn't he?" says Caine. "Like this sunset.

100

So calm, peaceful, serene," he says with a tinge of sadness. "It's such a shame that there are so many things that can ruin this sunset."

The woman continues to keep her eyes closed and turns her head. She speaks in a frightened voice. "Su ... such as ..."

Caine replies in a matter-of-fact tone. "Well, the weather for example. All it takes is a little rain and boom." Caine places his hand on the woman's shoulder.

She is engrossed with fear and cannot move. Her pulse begins to race and sweat beads upon her forehead.

The scene unfolds beneath the dimming hues of the sunset, tainted by Caine's menacing presence. His grip on the woman's shoulder tightens, ominous in its weight. "See, I want control over the weather. To make it obey my every whim," Caine muses with a chilling certainty.

"How ...how do you even do that?" the woman stammers, her nerves frayed and heart racing.

"It's simple, really," Caine responds slyly, relishing the fear. "You just take away its power."

Before the woman can finish her sentence, Caine swiftly absorbs her soul, a cruel display of his unearthly might. The woman's body slumps to the bench's side, lifeless. "Just like that," Caine murmurs, holding the woman's essence in his icy grasp. "Hmm, she's seen much, faced trials, but a good specimen nonetheless." His gaze lingers on the captured soul, then he slowly unfurls his jaws, ensnares the soul with his tongue, and devours it. "Sinfully delicious."

Caine stands to his feet, adjusts his cufflinks and begins to walk through the park. He observes the children playing and people enjoying each other.

He scoffs, "Look at all the people living in denial. Ignoring the truth of this world."

He sneers, his voice a venomous hiss. "Look at these people, living in blissful ignorance. Blind to the harsh realities of this world," he scoffs, drawing out his words with contempt. "They pollute this beautiful world, oblivious to its splendor. And what do they do? Breed, recycle their filth, and dump their decaying corpses into the earth! Utterly unruly creatures! When I reign, I'll dictate their fates, control their every move. I'll restore true balance, as Satan promised. I will be king, and I'll execute his mission!"

He continues to walk through the park, his disdain growing with each step, as he views humans doing everyday activities and normal things that give them joy. His disdain slowly fills his aura and with the nighttime slowly approaching, it causes his evil energy to grow. He walks by a man and woman having a conversation in a secluded area and pauses.

The man says, "You heard me right, you give me what I want, and I'll give you what you're asking for."

The woman replies, "That is despicable! How could you even suggest something like that?"

She continues, "I have worked hard for you for years, and this is how you treat me?!"

Caine focuses his attention on their words.

The man replies, "If you want the promotion, you'll do exactly what I want, right here, and no questions."

Caine interrupts with a question toward the woman. "Excuse me, is this man bothering you?"

"Hey, stay out of this, buddy!" exclaims the man placing his hands on Caine.

"You should try to stay out of her, my good man," says Caine with an evil smile sprawled across his face.

The man's lips purse, his eyes pierce at Caine and he grabs him by the collar. "Who the hell do you think you are?!"

Caine's eyes turn black as coal before the man; a sharp chill runs down his back. Fear and despair overwhelm him in an instant.

"Hell. I am hell."

In an instant Caine grips the frightened man by his head and begins to use the evil energy within him to fuel a hellish nightmare. His demeanor changes, fear and misery overcome his face. The woman looks on paralyzed in fear, the man begins to scream and Caine covers his mouth. "Oh now, none of that on this peaceful evening." The man experiences a heart attack and Caine absorbs his soul before he succumbs to it. Caine slowly looks at the woman. "Such evil deserves to die, don't you think?" Caine's words send a frightening chill down the woman's spine. Her body is begging her to move but her mind is frozen. Caine releases the man's body and it lifelessly falls to the ground.

"Now, my dear, can you keep quiet about what you just saw?" Caine walks toward the woman and she begins to cry. Caine stands before the woman and cups her face; she tries to scream for help but nothing comes out. "Just turn around and walk away and I promise you I won't lay a finger on you, my dear."

The woman slowly turns with tears rolling down her face. She takes a step forward and then another. She begins to feel as though she will make it home to live to see another day. In an instant Caine grips her shoulder.

"Thank you for taking those steps. You would've made a great subject to rule."

Before she can even utter a word, he absorbs her soul and she falls to the ground, lifeless. "But to be on the safe side of you stirring the pot." He turns back and looks at the man he sent into a homicidal nightmare, reaches into his suit pocket, takes out his wallet.

"Ah CEO, that makes things even MUCH easier." Caine stands over the man's corpse, holds his hand out over it and emanates a dark aura from his hand that covers the man's corpse and slowly Caine's face morphs into the very man he just killed. He then grabs his access card. "Now to really have some fun."

Caine instantly teleports to a nearby alley, close to the CEO's building, walks toward the front entrance of the building and scans the dead man's badge, gaining entrance to the building. He walks toward the front desk and speaks to the receptionist. She looks up and focuses her attention on Caine, not even realizing that her boss is no longer even in the body that stands before her.

"Hello, Mr. Matthews, how can I help you?"

"Yes, can you tell the board of directors that I would like to call an emergency meeting immediately?" he says with a smile.

The receptionist's face quickly shows an expression of concern. "Is there something wrong, Mr. Matthews, it's closing time, are you sure?"

"Oh no, no I just need to address something that may become a potential hazard to the company in the future, just a bit of damage control." She smiles back, begins typing at her computer and sends out an urgent email to the current board of directors.

"It's all set, Mr. Matthews."

"Thank you, my dear. You are truly ... dispensable." He walks toward the elevator and presses the button to go up.

"Mr. Matthews, you do mean indispensable?"

Caine replies with a smile as the elevator door closes behind him.

Caine enters the man's office, his eyes drawn to the array of family photos on the desk. His gaze lingers on them for a moment, a flicker of emotion crossing his face. Memories flood his mind, a hint of sorrow seeping into his features. He carefully adjusts the frames, a fleeting sense of connection evident. Then, with a sudden shift, he flips the photos face down. Before leaving, he envelops the room in dark energy, setting the pictures ablaze. The crackling flames engulf the room, shattering the serenity, and chaos reigns as the windows splinter under the immense force.

The boardroom buzzes with tension as Caine strolls in. "Ladies and gentlemen, please take your seats," he announces with a subtle smirk.

"What's the meaning of this interruption, Lawrence? I was in the middle of dinner with my family," protests one of the board members.

Caine chuckles, a hint of darkness in his tone. "It's not as if you truly cared about them anyway." He smirks. "I mean if you did, you would still be eating with your family now, wouldn't you? I mean FAMILY IS THE MOST IMPORTANT THING."

"What is the meaning of all this? Did you call us here just to chastise us?" questions another board member, trying to contain their frustration.

Caine leans back, an air of amusement about him. "No, not solely for that," he retorts. "I brought you all here to discuss business."

"Let me guess, is it the business of another sexual harassment claim," says another board member questioning his motives.

108

Caine snickers. "No, but that sounds fun. I'll add it to the list of things to get to. I called you here, because I wanted you all to know how I am proceeding forward with my company."

"Your company?!" replies a confused, angered board member. "You mean the company we've spent years building up in spite of your efforts to tear it down at every turn, with your outdated ideas and awful publicity?"

"The company that I started," rebuts Caine confidently.

"You started it, but you'll end it if you continue like this," retorts another member, frustration evident.

"He's wasting our time. Let's leave," says another board member, rising from their seat, signaling an end to the unproductive exchange.

As the board members begin to walk out, Caine stretches out his left arm and focuses it toward the room doors and slams them shut with his powers. He locks the door and turns his attention to the board members, who are at this point frightened beyond belief as they begin to realize that something about their colleague is completely off.

Caine emits a black and purple aura behind him. "You'll be taking your seats, now!"

Caine telekinetically forces all the board members into seats and places them around the boardroom table as everyone shrieks in terror as they are shifted around the room in a frenzy. Caine stands at the head of the table. "Now, our influence over this little piece of Earth is vast, we have the ability to affect so many things in this nation." He continues on. "Poverty, hunger, equality, health ... instead we choose to hoard our wealth, to continue our frivolous mission of money and power for some and nothing for most."

A board member speaks up in protest of Caine's speech. "What are you even saying?!"

Caine turns to look at the member and teleports behind him. He grabs him by the back of the head and slowly crushes his skull, killing the man, leaving his lifeless body to sit with his head tilted back while his remaining brain matter drips out of his open skull. "Please do not interrupt me."

The other members begin to scream and Caine forces their mouths closed. "That goes for all of you too. Now, where was I ... Ah yes." He walks back to the head of the table. "You have turned this company into a money-grubbing cash cow that only focuses on the needs of the people who sit right at this oversized table. Just last year you laid off five and a half thousand employees and didn't bat an eye or even provide a substantial severance to the employees you so easily let go. Utterly despicable."

The board members tremble with fear, a collective sense dawning upon them that this might be their final chapter. One board member lowers their head, closes their eyes and begins to pray in silence. Caine notices a shift in the energy in the room and looks toward her.

He walks over, grabs her jaw from the back. "Thoughts and prayers? They won't help you now," relays Caine making a sorrowful face. He grips her jaw and begins absorbing her soul. "Your soul is with me now." Her body goes limp and the other board member's muffled screams echo around the room. "I will be shifting the focus of this company and I will be using your bodies to keep up the facade that you're actually still alive."

"Even though the evil you've wrought will be remembered by those you've affected, now it will be resolved through your unwavering

111

kindness and charity over these next few days. This room will also serve as my base of operations for collecting souls and sowing chaos." Caine raises his hand above the entire table and one by one the souls of the board members who are still alive come into his hand, he absorbs them and their bodies go limp.

Caine looks up and notices that the door to the conference room has been cracked and the receptionist has been listening the entire time. She notices Caine's gaze affixed at the door and she turns to run but Caine stops her in her tracks and telepathically pulls her into the room screaming and into his hand. "So sorry, my dear, looks like curiosity will be killing the cat," he says while a subtle smile adorns his face.

"Wait! Please no don—"

Before she can finish, Caine drains her of her soul and throws her body on the conference table. He walks to the board member whose body he desecrated and repairs the body. "Could've had his soul too if I could've just controlled my temper, oh well it's not like it went to heaven anyway."

With a commanding gesture, Caine raises his hands, conjuring two ominous portals from which demons pour into the room, their eerie presence permeating every corner. His eyes fixate on the cityscape beyond the window, a sense of eerie determination enveloping his being.

"This time, it feels vastly different," he murmurs with an unsettling certainty. "I am destined to reign. I shall be their sovereign, their king. Nothing in this world will hinder my ascent." The building's floor quivers under a sinister aura as demons take flight, encircling the structure with an otherworldly menace. The air thickens with foreboding anticipation as his dark ambitions take shape.

Chapter 8: Highs and Lows

Two months later

The air is strange yet tranquil, carrying a delicate chill that hints at a forthcoming spectacle. Silence blankets the scene, the calm before the storm, until a gust disturbs the serenity, spiraling leaves into a wild dance. Suddenly two opposing elemental energies begin to dance, painting the air with a vibrant clash. Beams of radiant light intertwine with crackling bolts of lightning, creating a mesmerizing display. "OK, sis, keep up with me now!" Ray's voice rings out amid the chaos, a mischievous smirk adorning his face as he dashes in the opposite direction of Khalia. His words are carried away by the symphony of elements colliding in a breathtaking spectacle.

In perfect sync with her swift stride, Khalia counters Ray's strikes with unwavering determination. Her voice cuts through the intensity of their sparring match, charged with confidence and determination. "That ain't no problem!"

Ray's fists surge with luminous light energy, each strike aimed with precision, but Khalia remains resolute, harnessing her lightning energy to deflect his onslaught. Their clash is a mesmerizing display of elemental prowess.

"Push yourself, Ray! At this stage, subduing lightning should be child's play for you," Master Hue urges, his words carrying both challenge and encouragement, a testament to the two's shared quest for mastery over their formidable abilities. The air crackles with anticipation as their energies collide, each strike a testament to their unyielding determination to surpass their limits. Ray redirects the lightning away into the air and engages Khalia in close combat with his light energy. She is not one to be outdone; she begins to match Ray blow for blow, parrying his strikes and calculating his movements.

They surge forward, swift streaks of determination merging into a blur as Khalia and Ray intensify their clash, their movements transcending the ordinary eye's perception. Their energies intermingle, creating a vibrant tapestry of light and crackling lightning in their wake.

Meanwhile, across the field, the rest of the team engages in their own rigorous sparring sessions. Viera and Zeke engage in a graceful but fierce duel, their weapons weaving intricate patterns through the air, a dance of skill and precision. With calculated strikes and swift maneuvers, they hone their expertise, each movement refining their mastery of their chosen tools.

Dontrelle, wielding his formidable axe, and Vincent, wielding his kunai and chain, engage in a dynamic display of combat prowess. Their sparring is a harmonious blend of weaponry and elemental prowess, seamlessly intertwining their fighting styles. The air echoes with the clash of metal and the crackle of elemental forces as they swap between techniques, fluidly transitioning between their weapons and elemental abilities, each move a testament to their adaptability and skill.

In the span of two intense months of training, the team has undergone remarkable transformations. Khalia and Ray now wield their elemental powers effortlessly, seamlessly harnessing their energies without reliance on their weapons. Vincent and Dontrelle stand as formidable hybrids, having achieved mastery in both wielding their weapons and commanding their elemental forces, exhibiting a dual prowess that embodies their dedication.

Yet, among this progress, an obvious divide emerges. Ezekiel and Viera deal with their struggles to establish a solid connection to their elemental abilities. While they persist in utilizing their weapons to channel their energies, the frustration of this limitation weighs heavily on them both.

Ezekiel, once indifferent to his brother, now finds himself thrown by their shared inclusion in this vital task. His initial assumption that he alone would possess these powers shattered when Vincent also became part of this fateful team. The superiority of Vincent's mastery in both powers and weaponry compounds Ezekiel's feelings of inadequacy, ruining his confidence and his ability to control his own powers.

Comparably, Viera faces her own internal unrest. Accustomed to being the dependable go-to girl, she grapples with a new sense of displacement within the team dynamic. Her struggle intensifies as she witnesses her best friend, Khalia, and the others making strides alongside the perceived "savior of the universe." The shift from being the go-to support to operating within a structured team dynamic challenges her deeply, testing her adaptability and triggering a sense of unfamiliarity and doubt in her capabilities.

As the duo engage in their lightning-fast spar, the rest of the team stands in awe, their eyes straining to keep pace with the whirlwind of movement. Even their heightened senses struggle to capture the blazing exchange.

"They're moving so fast, I can't even keep up!" Dontrelle exclaims, voicing the team's collective disbelief at the blur of motions unfolding before them.

"Ugh, it's just beams of light fightin' each other," Zeke remarks, trying to act unimpressed by the scene before him.

Interrupting the electrifying spectacle, Hue's commanding voice cuts through the air, signaling an end to the lightning-swift match. In an instant, the streaks of movement halt, revealing Khalia and Ray, now human once more, panting from their endeavor. A shared glance and a smirk pass between them before a gesture of mutual respect seals their bout with a handshake.

"Damn good, sis!" Ray praises with a grin, proud of his teammate for keeping up.

"Why, thank you, my dear," Khalia retorts playfully as she strolls toward Viera, her confidence in full swing. "I think I'm really getting the hang of things," says Khalia as she snaps and lightning pops from her hand.

But amid the camaraderie, Viera's jealousy peeks through. "Girl, don't get so cocky, you'll fuck around and zap a bird in the sky," she teases, her envy thinly veiled.

The rush of change and growth floods Khalia's thoughts. "Two months ago, I felt aimless and lost. Now, I don't know, this experience has transformed me," she reflects, a spark of determination glinting in her eyes. "I think I'm going to tell my mom I want to switch my major to tech innovation. What do you think?"

Viera's attention wanders far from the conversation, lost in the labyrinth of her own thoughts. Her focus is a facade, a mask concealing the struggle to reignite her powers, a battle that gnaws at her confidence and chips away at her patience. Oblivious to Khalia's attempts to talk to her, she remains lost in her own mental anguish.

The rift between Khalia and her best friend weighs heavily on her, a nagging feeling that something has shifted between them. Despite Khalia's recent strides, matching Ray's pace and innovating new technology for the team's benefit, anxiety lingers in their friendship. Khalia has always been Viera's biggest supporter, yet she feels an unsettling absence of that same support reciprocated.

Resting against the solid trunk of a nearby tree, Khalia seeks solace in its embrace, yearning for a break amid the whirlwind of emotions. She exhales a heavy sigh, the weight of unspoken tensions hanging in the air around her, a silent plea for understanding and harmony to restore the cherished bond with her best friend. The impending training session looms, but for now, she seeks a fleeting moment of tranquility to collect her thoughts before training resumes.

Ray walks toward Vincent and pats him on the back, Vincent turns, a smile lighting up his features in response to Ray's greeting.

"Look at the water boy, coming into his own!" Ray teases, his voice filled with playful admiration for Vincent's progress.

Vincent chuckles, his laughter resonating throughout the air. "Well, Mr. Savior of the Universe, I see your quips are on point, but your technique could use a touch-up."

Ray raises an eyebrow, adopting a mock-serious tone. "Oh, really now?" He turns to Master Hue, seeking confirmation. "Hey, Hue, when we kick off the training session again ..." Ray points toward Vincent signaling his next sparring partner.

"Very well," Hue responds, a hint of amusement in his voice, knowing what is brewing.

Vincent's reaction is swift. "Oh, so that's how we coming at it?!" he responds, a playful challenge lacing his words.

"Just like that," Ray affirms with a grin.

Dontrelle walks over and chimes in, "Just know whoever loses, I got next."

"Yessir, Mr. Second-in-Command, sir!" Ray mockingly echoes in a soldier's voice.

Dontrelle pushes him lightly, and the group erupts into shared laughter, the camaraderie binding them.

Off on the side, Zeke stands with his arms crossed and a glare that could pierce through hell itself into Lucifer's lair. Ezekiel is used to being the center of attention and Ray has made strong bonds with the majority of the team; even his brother and best friend are becoming his friends. The sight grates against his nerves like sandpaper, a silent turmoil brewing within him as he watches the trio form tight-knit connections, leaving him feeling distanced and alone.

The tension hangs heavy between Ezekiel and Viera as he approaches her, a troubled expression etched across his face. "You know, there's something about Ray that I don't like," he confides in a hushed tone, his eyes fixed on the trio of Ray, Vincent, and Dontrelle.

Viera's face contorts with doubt. "Zeke, he's literally been chosen to save the universe, handpicked by God and he's been nice to all of us what ... could possibly ... be suspicious ... about him?!" Her frustration is palpable as she attempts to focus on honing her air-based abilities.

Ignoring her attempt to refocus, Ezekiel persists. "Look, V, I'm just saying what if this is all a test by God, to show me that I'M supposed to be the leader?" She continues to try to hone her power.

"Or ... your ego can't handle ... not being certain of attention ... for once?" Her words cut through the air, challenging Ezekiel's assumptions.

Ezekiel sucks his teeth. "Viera, it's not that I ... What the hell are you doin'?!"

Viera is standing in front of Ezekiel in a strange pose, attempting to control her power with very minimal success. "I DON'T KNOW, ZEKE! I HONESTLY DO NOT KNOW!" Her frustration gushes forward, mirroring her internal turmoil. "I'm so used to grasping things so quickly and I don't understand ... WHY ... MY POWERS ... DON'T WORK!"

Ezekiel makes a well-thought-out deduction. "Well you're air, air is calm, it's chill, so maybe when you relax, they'll work like they're supposed to?"

Viera goes quiet and stares blankly at Ezekiel. "So you saying I'm some angry Black woman?"

Ezekiel catches air of where this conversation could go and turns and walks off. "NOPE!"

Everyone gathers around before Vincent and Ray begin to spar.

Hue's directive sets the stage, outlining the strategies for the duel between elemental powers, "Ray, you will battle primarily using your elemental energy with your bō to supplement and, Vincent, you will battle switching between weapon and element, understood?"

Simultaneously they speak. "Yes, Sensei!"

The two ready their battle stances and Hue continues. "The last Elemental standing is the victor ... READY ... SET ...Supā!"

Ray instantly moves toward his opponent, Vincent sprints backward and creates a veil of water for defense. Ray swipes through this wall and advances, striking at Vincent with his staff. Vincent parries using the chain attached to his kunai.

Ray begins to pick up speed on his strikes and Vincent tries to parry them one by one, but in the midst of his countermeasures, Ray has snuck an energy ball behind Vincent to explode on impact. Vincent absorbs the blast and is sent flying in the air. Ray follows behind swiftly, flying past Vincent and positions himself to strike him in the air. In that moment Ray moves to strike Vincent, the latter wraps the chain of the kunai around Ray sending them both plummeting to the ground.

"Oh, whoa!" yells Ray as he scrambles to loosen the chain but struggles, he has no choice but to bring them both standing to the ground.

"Aight, that was cool," exclaims Ray taking notice of Vincent's quick thinking.

"Thanks!" replies an enthusiastic Vincent as he unravels the chain and kicks Ray back a few feet. Vincent then manipulates the air around him to conjure water, his hand movements flowing and precise. In an instant, he summons a water energy sphere and fires a geyser at Ray.

Ray quickly places his staff in front of him and surrounds his staff with light energy and the geyser splits in front of the staff and walls of water rush past Ray as he siphons his energy into the staff. Ray begins to struggle as the geyser's power intensifies. Vincent then tenses his other hand and begins channeling the split geyser into a giant water sphere. The sphere becomes almost as large as the battlefield. "Seeing as though you're getting tired, let's take this to my turf," Vincent challenges, manipulating the colossal sphere toward Ray, signaling a change in the battleground.

The tension in the watery cocoon intensifies as Ray struggles to maintain his breath within the seemingly infinite expanse of water. The thought flashes through his mind—this would have been an opportune moment to learn how to swim.

Vincent, with a calculated smirk, enters the expansive water sphere and taunts Ray playfully before launching into a relentless assault. Blows land with precision, knocking Ray around and causing him to lose control of his breath with each impactful strike.

Amid the chaos, a voice resonates within Ray's mind—Hue's voice, breaking through the tumult. "Ray, listen to me ..."

Ray is taken aback. "Sensei? How am I even—"

Before he could finish his thought, Hue's urgency cut in. "There's no time for that, listen ... You need to unlock the depths of your power to free yourself. Dig deep and unleash it, NOW!"

Gathering his focus within the swirling water, Ray centers his energy, and a revelation strikes—he could breathe in this aquatic environment by centering his energy. Vincent, noticing this newfound resolve, moves in for a decisive blow. Ray gathers energy in his body and just as Vincent closes in he stops him in his tracks and forces him back with an energy sphere from his hand.

Ray then builds energy surrounding his own body and unleashes it like a bomb from his core. The water sphere explodes, covering the area with water and forcing Vincent to the ground. Hue and the rest of the team gaze at Ray who is still suspended in midair; he soon drops to the ground as the light energy surrounding him fades out. Hue runs toward him past Vincent and the others.

Hue's concern for Ray's well-being lingers in the air as he inquires, "How do you feel?"

Ray, still reeling from the intense exertion, replies uncertainly, "I'm fine ... I think ... why?" His gaze meets Master Hue's probing eyes, sensing an unspoken concern.

"It's nothing," Hue deflects, his demeanor shifting to a more composed stance. "The victor!" With a proud stance beside Ray, he presents him to the team, eliciting a round of gleeful applause, although Ezekiel's applause was tinged with evident sarcasm as he gazes distantly into the trees.

Ray approaches Vincent, extending a hand to help him up as Vincent pouts. "Damn good fight," Ray compliments with a playful grin.

Vincent, still catching his breath, grins slyly. "I almost had you!"

"Yup," Ray agrees with a chuckle. "A few more seconds and I would've been done, I forgot you're just as fast as Lia when you're underwater."

As Ray pulls Vincent to his feet, they share a knowing fist bump, a testament to their mutual respect and the exhilarating challenge they had just shared.

Master Hue's final words echo through the air, punctuating the day's training session with a sense of achievement and purpose. "I am very pleased with the team's progress," he begins, his voice resonating with pride. "You've all become a formidable force in these past few months. Soon, you'll confront demons and ultimately face Caine himself. Until that day arrives, continue to hone your skills. Remember, you're part of something greater than yourselves, and together, you can achieve greatness."

The Elementals speak as a collective. "Yes, Sensei." The team concludes training for the day.

Viera turns around to speak as everyone walks toward the base to leave. "Hey, it's been a long day! A friend of mine's hit me up about a new bar opening tonight in Little Five Points, y'all wanna go out tonight and shake all this stress off?"

Khalia, eager to support her best friend, chimes in enthusiastically, "Oh my God, V! Yes! That's exactly what I need."

"What do you say, boys?" Ray responds before Zeke has a chance to.

"Aye I'm down! Lehgo!" Vincent exclaims ready to go out on the town and have fun.

Zeke interjects in an assertive tone, "I got a date tonight, so y'all have fun ..."

Ray persists, attempting to encourage Zeke. "Aww, c'mon, man, bring her out, I'm sure she wouldn't mind!"

Reluctantly, Zeke relents. "Yeah ... sure ... cool." His response is tinged with a hint of reservation, signaling his hesitant acceptance.

Master Hue's voice calls out to Ray as the group begins dispersing. "Raymond, please before you leave I need to speak with you."

"Sure, Sensei," Ray acknowledges, bidding the rest of the team farewell with a wave before retracing his steps toward Hue. "Hey, what's up?"

Hue's concern lingers beneath his inquiry. "How are you feeling?"

Ray, puzzled by the question, responds, "I feel fine, should I be feeling something ... else?"

"Oh, no, I was just curious after today's training," Hue clarifies.

Curiosity piqued, Ray probes, "Sensei, what was that earlier? How could I hear your thoughts?"

Hue explains, "What you experienced was telepathy. You can connect to others using your light energy and access their minds, enabling communication."

Ray's eyes widened in amazement. "So, I can hear anyone's thoughts?"

Hue elucidates, "Yes, any living being, except demons and Caine himself. Would you like to try it on me?"

"Uh, sure," Ray agrees hesitantly.

Hue guides Ray through the technique. "Focus your energy to the middle of your forehead and concentrate on your target."

Ray follows Hue's instructions, honing his concentration toward Hue. "Can you hear me, Ray?"

Ray nods, mentally acknowledging Hue's thoughts. "I'd like to try something," Hue proposes. "Focus your thoughts toward me."

Ray concentrates his thoughts, attempting to communicate with Hue. "Is this working?"

A smile creeps onto Hue's face. "Yes, excellent job. It took me months to master this, and you've grasped it in seconds. What's your secret, Ray?"

Ray replies confused by the question posed by his master, "To what, Sensei?"

"To your advancement, how are you able to grasp things in such a short amount of time?" Master Hue elaborates.

Ray contemplates for a moment before responding, "I think it might be my overactive imagination. I imagine what I want, and it happens." As if to demonstrate, he shoots a beam of light energy into the ground. "Or maybe it's because I've always wanted to be a superhero ..."

Hue inquires further, "Would you mind explaining?"

Ray walks off to the side of Hue and continues talking. "Y'know, everyone loves superheroes. They help people, they fight for people, and they ... make people's lives better." Ray pauses. "So ... everyone loves them and now

I get to do all of the things they do." Ray begins to use his powers to levitate back to Hue. "Which is great ... because for a long time ... I felt like no one ... liked me. And because I thought no one liked me, I thought that maybe"—Ray pauses— "I ... shouldn't be alive."

Concern etched on Hue's face, he questions, "Have you ever felt like not living, Ray?"

Ray stops levitating. "Yeah ... A lot of times. Like I didn't deserve to ... Like I wasn't meant to. People can really make you feel like you shouldn't exist ... so what's the point of existing, when there's nothing to exist for." Ray conjures light energy into his hand and stares at it. "I think God got to me at the right time. 'Cause now that I'm fighting for something, I want to stay alive and I want to give it my all. That's my secret, I just really want to help."

Master Hue intervenes with a heartfelt sentiment, breaking the solemn silence between him and Ray. "Ray, you should know that you matter just as much as any superhero. Even without all the suits and powers, even if you're not saving everyone, you still matter ... you still deserve to be liked."

Ray attempts to interject, but Hue gently halts him. "If you're striving to do right by others, you should still feel that you matter too."

A faint smile tugs at Ray's lips. "I know," he quietly acknowledges.

Hue, not entirely convinced, turns to Ray and poses a question. "Do you?"

Ray's gaze shifts downward, his thoughts wandering, before gazing off into the distance.

Hue breaks the momentary silence. "Go home, prepare for the night with your friends."

"Yes, Sensei," Ray replies, a mix of gratitude and contemplation evident in his voice. With a nod, he turns to leave, his mind filled with Hue's words, pondering their significance and seeking solace in the upcoming gathering with his friends.

Chapter 9: Drinks, Desperations and... Demons?!

Caine lounges in the desolate boardroom, his feet leisurely propped up on the desk amid the wreckage of the once-lavish space, bodies of the deceased board members strewn among the ruins. Within weeks, he had transformed the building into a stronghold, a sinister hub for his ominous designs.

"Preparations are nearly complete," Caine declares, rising from his seat and striding toward the balcony that offers a panoramic view of the city. His gaze sweeps over the sprawling metropolis. "All the souls I need to fuel the negative energy of hell are in storage."

With a chilling certainty in his voice, he continues, "In a matter of days, my earthly demise will be but a prelude. Once resurrected in hell, I shall ascend to rule alongside my Master, molding this world to my will."

Returning to the room, Caine gestures dramatically. "Now, let's test my allies, who shall join me in the forthcoming celebration."

Standing tall, he conjures a swirling dark energy sphere, crafting a portal that materializes from its depths. In an eerie silence, demons emerge from the yawning portal, gradually assembling into a small but formidable militia at his command.

"My brothers!" Caine's voice resonates with authority. "Go forth into the night! Claim souls and hunt down those who dare to oppose my vision for change!" His command is absolute. "Do not hold back!"

The assembled demons surge toward the balcony, leaping off the edge and descending into the shadows of the night. With an ominous purpose, they scatter into the city, their mission clear: to track down and confront the heroes who pose a threat to Caine's malevolent plans for the world.

* * *

Viera and Khalia walk into the club side by side in their best outfits, commanding attention as all eyes turn to admire their attire. Among the gathering, the guys are already there, as well as Ezekiel and his date who is bored to tears because Ezekiel's hatred for Ray is overwhelming his ability to focus on his game, that is until Viera walks up to the group.

"Daaaaammmnnnn, y'all look gooooood!" Ray exclaims with enthusiasm.

"Thank you, bro!" Khalia responds, visibly pleased. "Trelle, what you think?"

Dontrelle, impressed by Khalia's appearance, nods in admiration. "Well, I'm certainly at a loss of words," he compliments, acknowledging the elegance that both Khalia and Viera bring to the gathering.

"Aye let's go dance!" Vincent's sudden enthusiasm surprises everyone, prompting chuckles all around, even from Zeke. With eager anticipation, the group moves to the dance floor, ready to enjoy themselves.

After a spirited dance session, Ray and Vincent take a breather, settling at a bar table to cool off. "Dawg! I did not know you could dance like that!" Ray exclaims, impressed. "You were on fire bruh!"

"Well thank you, thank you; I mean it was my major when I WAS in college," Vincent shares with a hint of nostalgia.

"For real? Why haven't you taken it further?!" Ray's curiosity sparks the conversation.

"Before all of this happened," Vincent reflects, "I wasn't as confident as I thought I was. I really appreciate you, Ray, you helped me see my worth. Mastering my powers and growing stronger—it made me feel like I could conquer anything."

"That's really great, man," Ray responds warmly. "I'm really glad you made a change for the better." Vincent's comment about self-love and friendship resonates with Ray, who quietly absorbs the sentiments expressed.

"Just a lil' self-love, that's all ya need and a good friend!" exclaims Vincent with a smile.

Ray sits there taking in everything Vincent has said to him. Despite the progress and efforts he's made, Ray still grapples with lingering feelings of self-doubt and uncertainty, a clouded emotional landscape that persists despite the passage of time and personal growth.

Vincent's interruption brings Ray back from his thoughts. "Hey! I'm heading back to the dance floor. You comin'?"

"Nah, I'm good man, Ima chill for a minute," Ray responds casually.

"Kay, hit me up if you need anything," Vincent replies before dashing back to the lively dance floor.

Ray sits and realizes that what Vincent said about helping him become a better person, really put a smile on his face. It made him feel like a better person. It's at this moment, an insidious thought creeps into Ray's mind.

"What if I ... no, no I can't do that ..."

Ray turns his head toward Viera and watches her stare at Khalia and Dontrelle as they dance. Ray begins to read Viera's mind.

"Ugh, look at her, she's gotten even smarter and now she's got the most eligible guy on the team on her radar, damn!"

Ray's eyes widen—Viera's jealousy toward her supposed best friend comes as a surprise. His focus shifts to Khalia and Dontrelle.

"OK, girl, just keep it cool ... He is so fine and seems so sweet, but he's so quiet sometimes," Khalia muses.

Dontrelle's thoughts follow. "Wow, she's gorgeous. I wish I could introduce her to my parents."

Ray's attention then turns to Ezekiel who can be heard nearby. He is struggling to keep his date entertained.

"Aye, lemme get two shots," Ezekiel requests from the bartender.

"Look, baby, I think I'm just gonna go home." Ezekiel's date is starting to get tired of his lack of focus and recently his game had been completely off.

He tries to keep her entertained. "Aww, c'mon, baby, the night is just getting started!" exclaims Ezekiel with a flirtatious edge.

"Zeke, it's eleven thirty-five and I got to study for finals this weekend, I'm gonna head out," she says motioning to stand.

"Wait, wait, now what if I show you something special?" Ezekiel says attempting to entice his date.

"Special like what?" she asks curiously.

The shots Ezekiel orders are placed in front of them. He looks around to make sure no one's watching. Ray is behind them so he doesn't pay attention to him watching.

"How about a little magic?" Ezekiel places his hand over the shots and focuses his elemental energy, causing them to light on fire.

"Yeah that did it." Ray reads his mind.

"Nice trick, Zeke, see you later." She walks toward the exit and heads out of the door.

"Damn, man!" Ray walks over to Zeke and places his hand on his shoulder.

"Yo! Dude, what was that? You need to be more careful about who you use your powers around." Ezekiel turns his face up to Ray.

"Nigga, please what she gonna do? Report me to God?" scoffs Ezekiel.

"Look, man, I'm just warning you that ...," Ray tries to reason, but Ezekiel interrupts with a warning of his own.

"Oh a warning, well then let me warn you, Mr. Chosen Nigga, I am on to you." Ray adopts a confused look on his face as Ezekiel continues.

"Yeah, I saw where your eyes were tonight. I know what you're really about," Ezekiel retorts angrily, accusing Ray of something seemingly sinister.

Ray reads his mind and finds out exactly what Ezekiel is thinking. "Let me hear it come out of your mouth then," replies an angered Ray.

Suddenly a woman's screams break the tension between the two. Everyone in the bar runs outside to see the commotion. The Elementals swiftly gather by the bar and Khalia addresses the group, "If that's what I think it is, I think we need to shift gears."

Ray locks eyes with Ezekiel, signaling urgency. "C'mon!" Ezekiel reluctantly follows suit, trailing behind the rest of the group. The Elementals hurry outside, stepping into a scene of sheer pandemonium. People flee in panic as demons capture and feed on the souls of those they capture. Viera is in shock. "Oh my God, what do we do?"

Thinking fast, Ray steps forward with a plan. "Y'all, I'm going out there. I'm gonna run while my powers are active. I'll distract the demons—get all the civilians out of the area, then get to my location and catch up to me."

Dontrelle speaks up, "Ray, NO! Those things could kill you!"

"We've trained for this for months," Ray insists, his voice resolute. "Remember what Hue said—if they're ready, then WE'RE ready. Trust in yourselves and each other."

Without hesitation, Ray dashes out of the club onto the chaotic streets, leaving a luminous white streak in his wake. The feeding demons halt abruptly, their actions interrupted by Ray's sudden appearance and commanding voice.

"Hey! I think y'all forgot somebody!" Ray's exclamation echoes through the chaos, prompting the demons to screech in response. Panic sets in as Ray turns on his heels. "Oh, shit!" he screams, breaking into a sprint as the demons give chase.

Meanwhile, Dontrelle takes command of the team, rallying them together. "Alright, let's move! We've got to help everyone and then get to Ray!" The team mobilizes, rushing to aid the civilians left behind in the wake of the demonic horde's onslaught.

Ray maintains his pace, continuously looking back to see the relentless pursuit of the demons, fueled by their insatiable hunger for his soul. His light energy serves as a beacon, drawing them closer with every stride. Determined, he dashes toward a blocked-off section of the highway, turning to face an army of demons in hot pursuit.

"C'mon, guys, where are you—I'm—" Before he finishes his thoughts, a pinion swoops in and knocks him off balance, sending him crashing onto the pavement. The sensation of warm asphalt envelopes him as he clambers to his feet, assessing the dire situation. "Dammit, I've got no choice," he mutters to himself, assuming a defensive stance.

Surrounded by a growing number of demons, at least ten and counting, Ray attempts to keep track of their movements. The air hums with their malevolence as they close in on him. With a rush of energy, a demon charges directly at him, forcing Ray to engage.

"Ah!" Ray exclaims, channeling his focus onto the first demon, infusing his hands with radiant light energy. He punches it in the dead center and the demon screeches and disintegrates instantly.

"Oh, whoa!" Ray shouts triumphantly as another punch obliterates a drooling demon's head.

He charges mercilessly at the next demon, one by one they turn to dust. He tries to keep up, but the numbers continue to grow. Suddenly, a demon catches him off guard, hurling him backward. On the ground, Ray braces himself, resigned to facing the inevitable. "Well, at least I'll go out honorably," he muses, closing his eyes as the horde advances, ready to strike.

As the demons close in and pounce like lions to prey, they are all blown back by a strong gust of air. Ray turns to see the rest of his team behind him and Viera with her arms extended.

"UGH! Finally!" Viera exclaims, a mix of relief and frustration evident in her voice.

Rushing to Ray's side, Vincent and Khalia help him to his feet. "You good?" Khalia inquires.

"Yeah, I'm alright. Took out a good chunk of 'em, but got too cocky," Ray admits.

"Sorry we took so long. More civilians needed help than we expected," Vincent explains.

"It's all good. Let's get ready. They're starting to regroup," Ray says, scanning the demons as they begin to stand, preparing for another assault.

The team braces themselves, standing united against the near threat. "Y'all ready?!" Ray calls out.

"Let's go!" replies Ezekiel.

The team collectively stretches out their left hands to the side and imbues them all with their respective elemental energy. The energy is charged into their steel bracelets. In an instant, the team is all outfitted in their respective fighting suits. "Weapons!" Ray commands, and with collective energy, their weapons materialize in front of them, ready for battle.

The team, driven by Ray's command, moves forward, engaging the demon horde in combat. Dontrelle, utilizing his elemental prowess, shatters the asphalt to ensnare a group of demons before entombing them in an earthen cocoon, causing their disintegration. Khalia's swift kicks and bolts of lightning reduce multiple demons to nothingness while Viera and Ezekiel coordinate their strikes efficiently. Vincent and Ray continue their relentless assault, whittling down the demon numbers, yet the battle seems never-ending.

"Damn! They don't have any let-up," Viera shouts in frustration.

Ray rises into the sky to oversee the battle situation, witnessing the team's valiant struggle against the seemingly endless horde. A demon flies toward Ray at top speed and he stretches out his hand to blast it and it disappears.

"God, if I go out, I just go ...," Ray mumbles under his breath before calling out to the team. "Y'all stop fightin' and start runnin' this way!"

The team collectively looks up to see Ray flying in the opposite direction of the highway. They follow his lead. Behind them the horde advances, clawing, snarling, and reaching at them desperate to steal their souls and leave them as husks.

"Ray!" Khalia calls out, seeking guidance. "What are we doing?"

Ray commands, "Khalia, full power run in a circle around them as a collective; everybody else, fight to keep them encircled!" Khalia begins racing around the army at top speed. The team follows suit and knocks any demon into the circle she's creating.

"OK, I hope this works ... Guys, on my command, run behind the spot I'm hovering over," Ray says preparing a strike.

The team responds with head nods. Ray closes his eyes and charges his body with light energy. An overwhelming light radiates from his body and he begins to shake. He opens his eyes.

"Move!" he cries out. The team dashes behind him and he instantly drops into the depths of the horde. The demons begin to claw at him and in an instant Ray unleashes the full force of his light energy. His body glows bright and a wave of force emanates, disintegrating the majority of the demons within a two-mile radius.

The demons disintegrate in droves. Only a few are left behind and the team makes quick work of the remaining demons. Vieira strikes two with her tonfa. Vincent wraps up three of them with his kunai and chain, Khalia assists him by striking them with her nunchucks.

Ezekiel and Dontrelle work together and take out four demons with their sword and axes respectively. They search for Ray among the soot in the air. Vieira uses her powers and clears the air. Ray is face down and the team runs toward him. They stand over him and turn him over. He awakens with a gasp of air. His suit is tattered and worn from the scratches and the blast. The team lets out a sigh of relief.

Ray slowly rises and looks around. "We get ... all of them?" Ray questions as he holds his chest.

"Yeah ... I think so ... What should we do now?" Dontrelle asks the group.

"Maybe we should go back to base and talk to Hue, I didn't know a horde could be this much work," says Khalia.

Ray looks around, disillusioned and a faint ringing in his ears. He thought that that would have been his final act. Yet he still stands.

Khalia turns to Ezekiel. "Zeke, can you watch our six and make sure no demons follow us?" Zeke nods but is still upset with Ray and his rage festering. The team undo their transformations and begin the walk back to base. Ezekiel isn't paying any attention and is less focused on what's behind him. A lone demon, unnoticed, tails the team back to their base, its sinister presence hidden from view.

Chapter 10: Something Wicked This Way...

The team finally arrives back at base after a long walk and slightly broken spirits. They have been fighting demons individually the entire time during their training, never imagining that it'd take this much energy out of them. They seek out Master Hue and call his name. He appears from the base entrance.

Khalia, breaking the silence, humorously remarks, "Either we just knuckled up with an army of hulks, or those were the hardest demons in Elemental history."

Hue acknowledges, "My apologies, Khalia, I should've warned you that they may be stronger this time around."

"Why is that?" Dontrelle inquires.

Hue responds, "It could be due to the shift in the balance of good and evil. When the last team failed to destroy Caine it may have caused the shift in the favor of evil, which would mean, that the demons would be more powerful this time around."

The revelation leaves the team in a state of concern and disbelief.

Viera says with grave concern, "You said that the last team failed, wouldn't that be ... your team?!"

"Yes ... it would ...," replies Hue resentfully.

"Wait, I thought that your team stopped Caine, just like the team before," Khalia says noting the prophecy that was explained to them in the beginning.

As the group is speaking, Viera senses a change in the air. "Y'all wait ... there's something here ..." The team turns to see a Trek coming full speed toward them screeching.

Reacting swiftly, Ray stretches his hand out to form an energy projectile and launches it at the demon, disintegrating it. "I thought you were checking our six?" Ray and the team look at Ezekiel and he begins to explain but is interrupted by an ominous voice.

"Yes, but most fortunate for me, his incompetence led me here ..." A figure appears and a chilling dark energy that shifts the very atmosphere accompanies it. The team looks up to see a man standing across from the base.

"Johnathan Caine ...," says Ray, realizing that the person standing in front of him is no ordinary human.

"Grand deduction, little light," replies Caine walking toward the group. "So ... this is the new team that's supposed to FINALLY put a stop to me?" He continues, "Well, seeing as though you defeated my demons in record time, I came to see for myself, just what you have to offer in terms of battle."

The team looks toward Ray, awaiting orders. "He wanna fight, let's give 'em a fight." Ray continues, "Upsilon formation!" The team takes its stance.

"Hmm, why are these suits color-coded, are you supposed to be the Power Rangers?" quips Caine.

Ray cries out, "Let's go!" Khalia and Dontrelle make first connect with Caine using their elemental energies. Nothing fazes him.

"That was cute ...," replies Caine with a sneer as he grabs Khalia by the throat. He hurls her forcefully, causing her to collide with Dontrelle, sending them both sprawling and injured.

Viera and Ezekiel try striking with their weapons but it's an even more futile effort.

"Absolutely pitiful!" With a single swift motion, he delivers a devastating blow to their stomachs, then seizes them by the heads, ruthlessly slamming them into the unforgiving ground.

Vincent's series of water strikes, though skilled, are effortlessly shrugged off by Caine. "This one," he comments, appraising Vincent, "shows promise." With a few consecutive punches, Caine renders Vincent defenseless, ultimately humiliating him by simply pushing him over with one finger.

Ray looks out at his defeated team and an anger builds that he had never felt before. He lunges at Caine and connects a blow using his bō.

"Ouchhhhhh, did that ACTUALLY sting a little?" Caine teases as he chuckles. "Tell me, little light, is your team the fuel for your resolve?" Caine grabs Ray by the collar and whispers in his ear. "Because you need a bit more to go toe to toe with me ..." Caine begins an onslaught against Ray. He strikes Ray directly in the face and then with a succession of right and left hooks.

Ray tries to put up a good defense by using his bō staff to block hits, but it is instantly slapped away. Caine punches Ray in the chest near full strength and sends him flying into the tree nestled in the edges of the training grounds.

"Ahh!" exclaims Ray painfully, making an impact. Ray tries to stand but there is pain coursing through his body from Caine's powerful punch.

"Can't even withstand one punch … How unfortunate … I thought you were all different, but it seems my deduction was completely unfounded," Caine sneers as the team struggles to stand. His voice drips with malice, each word a venomous taunt. "So, in a few days we were supposed to 'end' all of this. Then my reign will be set in stone; I will claim this world for mine once the balance has shifted in my Master's favor. I will rule as king." His eyes gleam with sinister intent, savoring the fear he's sowing.

"Well, seeing as though I've probably frightened you to your bones, let's make this even more fun. You all will face off with me in five days. Meet me at eight o'clock in the park to begin the festivities," Caine mocks with a chilling grin. His voice echoes a disturbing certainty. "If no one shows, I will find one of you and kill someone you love. Goodbye, Elementals," he announces with a chilling finality before vanishing into the shadows, leaving the team reeling with a sense of foreboding and dread.

Pain courses through everyone's bodies. The team regroups around Master Hue, their weary appearance revealing the toll of the encounter. Dontrelle, nursing his wounds, breaks the uneasy silence, seeking clarity amid the chaos. "So ... I'm gonna say that since the balance has shifted, Caine is a lot stronger now too, huh?"

Hue, his voice carrying a sense of remorse, acknowledges their concerns. "Yes, I regret not informing you sooner about this. I prioritized pushing your limits in training, neglecting to disclose crucial information."

Extending his hands, radiant with light energy, Hue uses his healing powers to mend the team's injuries. "The light energy possesses a healing ability, a fact I withheld to push you further, to encourage resilience in the face of adversity."

As he leads the team back toward the base, a somber tone in his voice, Hue reveals more unsettling truths. "Our base can be relocated to safeguard its secrecy, preventing Caine from discovering its whereabouts. A demon's inadvertent guidance led him here." His gaze falls on Ezekiel, who averts his eyes, the weight of guilt evident in his expression. "And lastly, my previous team ... they didn't succeed in fully suppressing Caine's power ..."

* * *

The night hangs heavy, a tense stillness enveloping the air as vibrant elemental energies clash fiercely with the darkness. Amid the exhaustion, the previous team valiantly confronts Caine after defeating the demons, their fatigue palpable yet their determination unyielding. Hue, driven by a desperate resolve, spots an opening and charges forward, channeling his light energy into a powerful strike. It seems to stagger Caine momentarily, but his recovery is swift and complete.

"Nothing's working ... Hue, what do we do?" queries the former Elemental of Air, a note of desperation tainting their voice. Hue, burdened by the weight of the situation, grapples with the magnitude of their predicament, the weight of the world pressing down on his shoulders. Faced with no other choice, he reluctantly issues the order. "Final gambit. Omega formation," he declares with a heavy heart.

The team shares a silent, solemn acknowledgment, swiftly aligning themselves in a strategic formation. As Hue harnesses his elemental energy to restrain Caine with a luminous beam, each member charges their powers and hurtles toward Caine, their bodies disintegrating upon impact, dissolving into the ether one by one until only Hue remains. Charging himself with intensified light energy, he propels himself forward, every fiber of his being in turmoil. Yet, amid the chaos, a singular word pierces through his thoughts—LIVE.

With a decisive shift in power, Hue throttles down his energy and surges toward Caine at breakneck speed, colliding with a blinding explosion. In the aftermath, barely conscious and grievously wounded, Hue lies amid the debris, a testament to survival. Struggling to rise, he scans the haze of smoke to find Caine standing threateningly before him, a chilling grin etched across his face. "That ... wasn't ... ENOUGH," Caine taunts with a slow disintegration, a sinister laughter echoing into the night.

※ ※ ※

"The omega formation is the Elemental team's last resort against an unstoppable force," Hue continues with a heavy tone. "I failed to fulfill my assigned destiny. The balance shifted, and I faced the wrath of a higher power. I was healed and secluded, awaiting the arrival of the next team."

Ray interjects, "Our team …"

Hue turns to them and affirms, "Yes, I was tasked to train you for the ultimate purpose—to vanquish Caine with the Crown of Thorns."

"So, you mean to tell me that this is all a big suicide mission?!" Dontrelle's disbelief echoes in the air. "No team has EVER beaten him, they just subdue him until the next few hundred years passes?!"

"That is correct, Dontrelle," Hue confirms.

"OK, this is a lot ... I don't know if we can do this," Vincent admits, a note of uncertainty in his voice.

"OK, I need to know, how bad REALLY, is a shift in the balance," asks Khalia seeking clarity. "What year was it when was the last one happened with your team?"

Hue laments slowly, "1525 ..."

"OK, well, what happened in 1525?" asks Ray, his curiosity piqued.

"Oh my God." Dontrelle's jaw drops at a shocking revelation and a chill runs down his spine. "The ... the Atlantic Slave Trade was in 1526. Your failure led to slavery and God punished you by assigning you to train us ... "

The weight of that revelation hangs heavy on the team, their shock evident. Ray senses their turmoil, grappling with his own fears before finding his voice amid the tension. "Y'all, I ain't gonna lie, I'm scared as fuck. This is beyond anything of what I thought it would be, so I wouldn't blame any of you for not continuing on with me."

The team is taken aback by Ray's unexpected admission. "Ray, what are you saying? We can't just—," Vincent begins, interrupted by Ray's determined gaze.

"Vincent, I get it, but this is bigger than us and I believe there is a way to end this all." Ray turns to Hue, seeking assurance. "The crucifix, if we execute it with the Crown of Thorns, could we put an end to this, once and for all?"

Hue replies, "I firmly believe that the crown and the crucifix are powerful enough to end him."

"OK then, if you guys want, you can stay and train with me. I really think we can do this together," Ray rallies, his resolve cutting through the uncertainty. "'Cause it's better than not trying at all; who knows what happens if the balance shifts in evil's favor for good. I don't wanna let that happen knowing I could've done something about it." Nearly all of the team looks at each other reluctantly and begins to follow Ray to the training area.

"Fuck ... NO!" Forceful exclamation cuts through the air.

Dontrelle reacts swiftly to Ezekiel's outburst. "Zeke man, what the hell?!"

"No, Trelle! Fuck all of this shit, and I mean that! Y'all sitting up here about to follow this nigga into battle with a mothafucka who just mopped the floor with us?! I am not following y'all into battle, especially with a nigga like HIM leading US!" Ezekiel's voice booms with frustration and anger.

Ray spins around, his expression shifting instantly, patience wearing thin as anger brews within him.

"Zeke, what the hell are you talking about?" Viera's voice cuts in, her confusion evident.

"Oh you ain't realize that this nigga's been reading our fuckin' minds?" Ezekiel's accusation hangs heavily in the air. "Or is it the fact that he's a fuckin' faggot?!" Ray snaps and moves at his fastest, closing in on Ezekiel with his weapon inches from his face.

"Listen to me carefully." Ray's voice is rigid with anger. "I know your brother allows for you to talk to him any kind of way ...but that word, from your mouth, aimed at me ... will get you KILLED ..."

Ezekiel stands, visibly conflicted, hands raised in a sign of surrender. The rest of the team steps back, concern etched onto their faces. Ray's sudden shift in demeanor has everyone taken aback. Dontrelle inquires gently, "Ray, it doesn't really matter but ... are you?"

Ray drops his guard, and he admits, "Yeah ... I am ... ever since I was twelve ..." Ray looks away with a rush of emotions flooding his senses. "It's something you kinda can't control, even when people force the notion down your throat that you can," Ray says angrily looking toward Ezekiel.

"Well, that doesn't matter to us ... Well 'US' anyway, but why did you read our minds?!" exclaims Khalia.

Ray's vulnerability surfaces as he turns to Khalia. "I'm not perfect, Lia, and honestly I did it because ... I wanted to know what you guys think of me. I'm insecure but at least I can admit that." Ray pauses, turns to Ezekiel and tilts his head. "Can you say the same?"

Vincent remarks softly, "Ray ... I guess I understand, but that's kinda messed up ..."

Ezekiel chimes in, echoing Vincent's sentiment. "Tuh, you got that right, bro!"

Ray responds with a pointed reply, "Oh! Look at YOU! COMMUNICATING with your brother! I'm so very proud of you!" Ray walks toward the battlefield, frustration sprawled across his face. "Hey, I have a GREAT idea. You think you can lead this team? I tell ya what, you beat me in a sparring match. You can lead the team and I will follow every SINGLE order you give!"

Ezekiel looks at Ray with determination in his eyes. "Alright, Ray, now you talkin'!"

Viera addresses Ezekiel, "Zeke, are you sure about this?!"

"Yeah, V! I got this!" Ezekiel responds confidently.

Ray interrupts with malicious intentions, "Yeah, V, he got this! You sit over there and figure out why you're so jealous of your 'BEST FRIEND'!"

The rest of the team swiftly looks toward Viera in confusion.

Ray exclaims, "Yeah, girl, you might wanna have a conversation with your sister!"

"V! What the hell?!" exclaims Khalia, shock and confusion adorning her being.

Viera looks away and down, ashamed of what Ray has pointed out. Ray continues his warpath as he prepares to spar. "Hue, you wanna call this?"

Master Hue replies with concern, "Ray, I do not think this—"

"Fine, Zeke, first Elemental to put the other on their ass, WINS! " exclaims Ray setting the rules for the match.

Zeke gets pumped and stands ready to fight. "Aight, let's go! Trelle, count us off!"

In the charged atmosphere, Dontrelle reluctantly begins the countdown. "Three ... two ... one ... Supā." The fight begins. Ezekiel rushes toward Ray, his punches aimed but futile as Ray effortlessly dodges each one. Ezekiel continues to throw punches and is unsuccessful in all efforts as Ray easily dodges them. "C'mon, fight back," exclaims a frustrated Ezekiel.

With his patience now completely exhausted, Ezekiel tries to use his elemental fire power. He musters all the elemental energy he has into his right fist and uses a powerful strike aimed at Ray's face.

But as the blow connects, Ray remains unfazed. He calmly remarks, "You done? Good."

Suddenly, Ray unleashes an onslaught against Ezekiel, landing blow after blow. Ray punches Ezekiel in the stomach sending Ezekiel staggering. He then punches Ezekiel dead in the face and his nose begins to bleed. The team looks on with concern and fear.

Ray begins to talk as he's pummeling Ezekiel. "Hey, Zeke! I think I know what your problem is with your power." Ray grabs him by the collar just as Caine had done Ray. "Fire isn't ANGER, it's PASSION, and YOU'RE SERIOUSLY LACKING!" Ray continues his assault; he punches Ezekiel giving him a black eye. "You're not passionate about ANYTHING! Love, life, family, especially family! Look at the way you treat your own flesh and blood!"

Ray pauses and holds Zeke in the air using his light energy. "The problem with niggas like you, Zeke? You hate yourself, so of course you can't love anyone else. You don't respect yourself, so you can't respect anyone else and if you had any sense at all you'd take notice, that someone is RIGHT HERE for YOU if you just stopped being a dick!" Ray slams Ezekiel down to the ground on his back effectively ending the match. Ezekiel lays beaten on the ground struggling to stand up.

"You, Zeke?! You are the worst of us! You judge someone like me, because I dare to be my best self, while you hide from what you could be! You hurt the people who love you, because you're fearful of their rejection and you think you can lead when you have absolutely, NO LEADERSHIP IN YOU." Ray moves his staff to come down on Ezekiel; in the nick of time, Vincent stops Ray using his chain.

"Ray! I think he gets it," Vincent interjects with his kunai and chain wrapped around Ray's staff, his face adorned with worry and assurance. Ray pauses and looks down at Ezekiel struggling to get up; feeling the parallels of Caine just beating the team, he turns away and walks away from the group.

Master Hue approaches Ezekiel to heal his wounds. Ezekiel gets just enough healing light to stand, looks at the team, turns and runs away. Dontrelle looks at Ray and then follows Ezekiel out.

Khalia looks at Viera perplexed. "V?"

Viera is too ashamed to speak, she begins to tear up and she runs as well. Khalia and Vincent stand and look at each other.

Vincent turns to address Ray. "What do we do now?"

Chapter 11: Fade to Black

Four days later ...

Days had passed without the team talking to each other. Ray directed Khalia and Vincent to go and check on their family and friends while Hue and Ray stay behind. Hue begins teaching Ray the crucifix, who is trying to do it on his own using the Crown of Thorns, while learning the technique for completing it. However, he learns that all the team needs to be a part of the act. "This is going to be hard if it's just me, Sensei," says Ray.

Master Hue replies, "Yes a trial indeed, but maybe we can work together." Hue continues, "I would be honored to fight alongside you, Ray. In such a short time, I've seen you become something more than what most teams could only dream to see."

Ray laments, "Yeah, well what about a few days ago?"

Master Hue offers wisdom. "Raymond, you fell a little short, but just because one falls short, it does not mean that one deserves to fall away. Mistakes are meant to be made. It's how you handle your mistakes when it comes time for resolution." Ray takes solace in Hue's words.

Amid their conversation, Ray's phone rings, his mother's name flashing on the screen. He picks up with a mixture of surprise and hesitation.

"Uh ... hello ..."

"Oh, Ray?! Ray baby, is that you? Thank goodness you answered!"

"What's wrong, Mama?"

"Oh nothing, baby! I am in town and I wanted to see if I could see your face?"

"Oh well, um ..."

"Ray, I understand if it's a no, God knows I don't deserve a yes," Ray's mother says.

Ray pauses, considering her feelings. "No, Mama, it's OK! Umm, hey how about we go to the mall, you remember how much fun we had shopping back in the day? Let's do that again."

"Oh wonderful, absolutely wonderful. OK, meet me at The Lenox Mall!"

"OK, Ma, I'll see you there."

"OK, baby, I'll see you soon."

Ray turns back to Master Hue. "I know this is the last night but if someone is gonna die at eight then—"

Hue interrupts with understanding. "Go and see your mother; be back here by seven thirty."

Ray nods and rushes off, leaving Hue to watch him depart before heading back to the base, contemplation etched on his face.

* * *

Vincent arrives at Ezekiel and Dontrelle's house, hesitating before knocking. Ezekiel opens the door, greeting Vincent with a quizzical look.

"Vince?" questions Ezekiel.

"Hey, bro, I didn't know you knew I was here …," Vincent stumbles.

"Saw you on the camera ..." Ezekiel chuckles.

"Oh ...," Vincent replies nervously.

"You wanna come in?" questions Ezekiel.

"Oh! Yeah ... sure," Vincent replies as he walks in and stands opposite Ezekiel as he closes the door. Ezekiel turns off the TV and Dontrelle stands out of view in his room, nudging Ezekiel to speak to his brother. They stand there in silence; Ezekiel is at a loss for words until Vincent breaks the tension.

"Hey ... uh ... are you OK ... from ... the other day?" Vincent asks, sensing Ezekiel's unease. Ezekiel turns away and looks down. Vincent believes he's still raw about the situation, Ezekiel turns to Vincent with teary eyes.

Ezekiel, visibly emotional, questions Vincent. "What's up with you, man?"

Vincent looks on with concern. "What do you mean, Zeke?"

"Bro, you come here to check up on me? After everything I said to Ray? After the way I treated you?! How do you still make space for me?" Ezekiel asks confused at Vincent's capacity to love.

Vincent replies, "Zeke, I'm your brother alright, no matter how much you push me away, I'm gonna ALWAYS try and be there for you." Ezekiel walks to the couch and sits down. He motions for Vincent to join him.

Ezekiel opens up to Vincent. "Vince ... I need to be real with you. When you came out, it was kinda hard for me too."

Vincent's face is muddled with confusion.

"I know it was about you and how you felt, but Mom, Dad, the church, they all rallied around you. They protected you, they loved you, even more ... even more than me."

Vincent interrupts, "Zeke, c'mon, man, that's not true."

"Yes it is, Vince, they took the love they had for both of us and put it all in you." Ezekiel repositions his body on the couch. "Then when Trelle came along, I felt like a brother again." Vincent recalls a memory of their lives, while Ezekiel overexaggerates; Vincent can remember times where his brother may have felt more neglected within the family.

Ezekiel speaks with his head down, recalling his emotions. "I felt so left behind sometimes, like nobody cared, so that's why I turned into what I turned into ... but in truth, you always cared, YOU never left my side, bro, and I see that now. It just took an ass whooping to set me straight."

The two look at each other and Vincent chuckles. Then Ezekiel chuckles, soon they are sharing a full-blown laughing session. "Dog, I had NEVER seen Ray like that!" exclaims a laughing Vincent.

"Bruh, he was gonna take me clean out!" exclaims a laughing Ezekiel. They both slowly come down from laughing. "Thank you for saving me, again ... Big bro," Ezekiel says softly.

Vincent replies empathizing with Ezekiel, "Anytime, lil' brother."

Dontrelle exits his room smiling, "'Bout time you dudes make up!" He grabs them both and hugs them tight.

"Aye, man! Get off of me!" Ezekiel laughs as they separate.

"Aight, aight, but real quick, you guys realize it's the last day right," Dontrelle reminds them.

Vincent and Ezekiel look at each other and nod their heads. "Let's go. If Caine takin' one of us out, then he takin' all of us out," Ezekiel announces sternly.

With resolve, they leave the house, heading toward the base, ready to face the imminent challenge together.

* * *

Khalia is in the midst of cleaning her room when her mother walks in.

"Hey …," says Khalia's mom.

"Oh hey, Mama, what's up?" replies Khalia, slightly distracted.

Khalia's mom sits on her daughter's bed and taps it to gesture for her to come sit. "C'mere, baby."

Khalia sits next to her mother. "Now for the past few months you been on cloud nine; now the past few days you been moping around and acting like the world is coming to an end."

Khalia's darts her eyes wondering if her mother had figured out that she had become a superhero.

"What's wrong, honey?" she asks, noticing Khalia's unease.

"Uh ...V and I had a, well ... I wouldn't say a fight." Khalia pauses. "I found out for the past few months, she's been feeling jealous of me. We joined this new team and I've been kind of thriving in it and she's been a little behind."

"Well I think I could understand how she's been feeling," replies Khalia's mother. "When I was in school, your Auntie Carolyn was thriving in every subject except political history. I thrived there and she struggled, which put a strain on our relationship. I'd offer to help and she'd refuse every time. It wasn't till after our first exam, where she finally realized she needed my help and came running for it, I know she was hurt by that. Sometimes admitting that we're not perfect can really put a drag on ya self-esteem and can mess with the relationships with the people around us. Viera's just dealing with the fact that she's not perfect at everything, she'll come around eventually," Khalia's mom says reassuring her.

Khalia embraces her mother and then stands to speak to her. "Mama, I ain't perfect neither, I don't want to major in political science anymore, it's not where I wanna be; to be honest I want to go into computer science and I been feeling that way for a while now," Khalia admits, nervous about disappointing her.

"I am so glad you finally said something, oh honey!" her mother reassures her, showing immense support for her decision.

"You're not mad?" Khalia questions assuring that her decision is OK.

"Absolutely not! I think it's wonderful you wanna follow in your daddy's footsteps!" exclaims Khalia's mom excited for her daughter. Khalia looks away to prevent herself from crying.

"Listen, if you ever want to talk about ANYTHING, you know I'm here for you," Khalia's mom reassures her.

Khalia replies comfortably, "Thanks, Mama."

Khalia's phone pings. She picks it up and it's the camera out front. "Well, would you look at that, technology bringing us together already?"

Viera lingered outside Khalia's door, her nervousness intense as she awaits Khalia's response to the doorbell. Khalia hugs her mom goodbye and hurries downstairs, her anticipation evident. As she opens the door, she finds Viera standing there, her apprehension clear in her voice.

"Hey ...," Viera says, her tone reflecting her worry.

"Hey!" Khalia responds cheerfully, masking her own concerns. "How are you?" she asks, trying to ease the tension.

"I'm OK, you?" responds a nervous Viera.

"I'm good," Khalia replies, leading Viera to a garden bench in the front yard. "Come sit and talk to me."

Viera joins Khalia on the bench, her discomfort apparent as she fidgets, avoiding eye contact. Khalia, in a gentle yet firm tone, encouraging her to open up.

"Girl, just talk to me, c'mon now."

Viera turns to Khalia, her words hesitant but sincere. "I really don't know what to say, except that I'm sorry ..."

Khalia, folding her arms, prods gently. "For?"

"For ... being jealous of you?" Viera responds quietly.

"Girl, I'm not upset with you for being jealous of me! It's everything surrounding it!" Khalia replies, recounting moments of passive-aggressive behavior. "You being passive-aggressive, not listening to me, ignoring me so you don't have to see me."

Viera hangs her head, realizing the accuracy of Khalia's words. "Lia, you're right, I have been awful toward you," Viera confesses, remorse coloring her voice. "I am sorry for everything I've done and made you feel. Girl, you're my best friend; hell, girl, you're my sister. You deserve much better than that."

Khalia gazes at Viera earnestly and forgives her, pulling her into a tight embrace. "Apology accepted, girl." They hold on to each other, relieved to have cleared the air.

"V, look, let's promise from now on if EITHER of us is feelin' a way about the other, we will BOTH discuss it, aight?" Khalia proposes.

Viera agrees with a smile, sealing their promise with another embrace.

Khalia shifts the conversation, trying to lighten the mood. "OK, you ready to go possibly die?"

Viera, her mind heavy with thoughts of Ray's relentless training, faces the harsh reality of the impending danger. "Yeah, I thought about Ray and I just know he ain't stopped training and this is the last night, one of us is supposed to ... die."

Khalia extends her fist playfully. "Or we could live!"

Viera, acknowledging Khalia's attempt at humor, resolves to face the challenge together. "OK, girl, c'mon, let's go."

* * *

Ray arrives at the mall and sees his mom standing by the entrance looking for him. She spots him and shouts his name. "Ray baby?! Is that my big baby?"

Ray replies with a chuckle, "Ha, yeah, Mom, it's me."

"Oh, my baby!" Ray hugs his mom and tries to adjust to her energy, their previous exchange leaving him tense and defensive now, but his mother's demeanor is different. She's much more open and caring at this moment. He starts to ponder, is something wrong? Is this all a facade to get hit with bad news later? He continues and his mom suggests they go in.

* * *

Two hours later ...

Ray and his mom leave a store, hands filled with bags of items. They smile ear to ear, laughing about how cute Ray looks in an outfit they both pick out together. The last few hours feel like they've never had a lapse in communication. Ray feels like he has someone to support him again and genuinely loves him, but a looming thought remains in his head. Why is his mom showing up now?

They stop walking when they get to the food court and take a seat. Ray's mom goes to get them some pretzels and joins Ray at the table.

"Oh, you know I love these pretzels, they are so damn good," exclaims Ray. "I know they have been your favorite since you were five, from the first time I brought you to the galleria in Birmingham." Ray looks up surprised. "I can't believe you remember that."

"I could never forget that day. We had been shopping all morning, and we stopped at the food court and I got you your first pretzel, and you had the biggest smile on your face since I think you had been born." Ray smiles. "Yup, just like the one on your handsome face right now." Ray smiles harder and chuckles.

"Then, we got in the car and drove home; you slept with a smile on your face the whole way," she says fondly ending the memory.

"Mama ...what's going on?" questions Ray. "We haven't spoken since ... I can't even remember when. Is something going on, what's wrong?"

Ray's mom looks at him with sadness in her eyes. "We haven't talked since ... you came out to me ..." Ray looks down. Recalling that memory makes him tense up and a chill runs down his spine, an uneasy feeling rises in his stomach.

"Ray ... I have been trying to talk to you for a while now, but I thought I needed to say this in person ..." Ray awaits to hear his mother's judgment once again as before.

"I wanted to apologize, Ray," replies his mom.

Ray drops his guard and a wave of relief covers his body. He's in shock, he had never heard his mom apologize for ANYTHING before.

"Recently, I had a wakeup call, I almost thought ... I thought I wasn't going to be here, but it made me think about you." Ray's mom pauses and looks at him. "I went to the church and learned some new things from a new pastor, opened up YouTube to watch some things and I learned ... you are who you are and ... that doesn't change a thing about WHO you are. I firmly believe that God still loves you and if he can love you, I damn sure should be able to love you too."

Tears stream down Ray's face, his mother offering comfort. "Are you OK, baby?" Ray's mom asks as she cups his face and wipes his tears away.

Ray smiles and responds through his sniffling, "Yeah, Mama ... I'm OK, Mom, I'm just fine." Ray begins to think about how his actions have pushed the other good people in his life away just as his mom did.

"Aye, Mama, I need some advice," Ray continues. "I'm uh ... I'm working on this new 'project' for work and it's been pretty rough. The team I'm working with ... we had a huge argument and I think I hurt some feelings in the process but now, I don't know how to go about fixing things ..."

Ray's mom tilts her head. "That's my baby, I know you probably put up with a lot from the group before you finally unleashed Raymond, huh?" Ray chuckles and nods in agreement. "Listen, baby, you know as well as I do sometimes all it takes is an apology. If the team really cares, they'll accept it and you'll be able to work a bit better with each other after everything is said and done."

Ray smiles and replies, "Thanks, Mama ... whew OK wait, this pretzel is REALLY salty." Ray winces at the salty exterior meeting his taste buds and stands up. "I'm gonna get us something to drink."

Ray's mom chuckles. "Ha ha, OK, baby, I'll be right here."

Ray walks over to order drinks from the closest restaurant to the table. He's ecstatic and elated. His mom is back in his world and even more loving and understanding than before. All he can think about is how much he can't wait to talk to her more and how much things will be easier on him having someone to talk to who understands things. As he's thinking about the future he's not paying attention as he's walking and bumps right into someone walking across his path.

"Oh! Oh my God, I'm so sor ... Qasim?!" Sure enough it was Qasim, doing some shopping and getting ready to head out of the mall.

"Dude, what are you doing here?" questions Ray.

"What do you mean what I'm doing here? It's the mall, I came to buy something," quips Qasim.

They share a laugh. "What are you doing here?" asks Qasim.

"Oh, shopping with my mom, man. She and I hadn't talked in a while but she reached out to me and we met up here and we had a really good time and then, she told me that she accepts me for who I am."

Qasim's eyes widen, he didn't even know that Ray was gay. He smiles and then congratulates him on his familial reunion. "I think that's great, man, I haven't talked to my parents in who knows when …," laments Qasim recalling his own familial struggles.

Ray interjects, "Well my mom had been reaching out, I've just been ignoring her because of our past and with me being really busy recently."

"Oh, you mean the whole saving the balance of good and evil in the universe thing," responds Qasim.

Ray begins to speak, "Yeah, man and then ... WAIT WHAT HOW DID YOU KNOW ABOUT THAT?!"

Qasim calms Ray and explains, "It's all good, it's all good, I'm not gonna tell anyone OK? Zeke told me a while back. It was also strange when you just stopped coming to work one day, I just put two and two together and ..."

Ray rolls his eyes and drops his head. Of course Zeke went blabbing about everything he possibly could. "Listen, y'all's secret is safe with me."

Ray gives a sigh of relief. "Thanks, man, say you got the time? I left my phone on the table."

Qasim replies, "Oh, it's almost eight."

Ray's heart drops to his feet and a chill surges through his body. He had forgotten all about where he was supposed to be at eight o'clock. He turns toward his mother and in an instant everything around him is coated in black and is frozen solid. He can barely move a muscle and tries to walk toward her but it feels like gravity is holding him back. What is this, he thinks to himself. Once again as before, a malevolent energy comes flooding in.

"Hello, little light ...," says Caine as he enters the mall court. "Do you like my little parlor trick? It's new! I'm granted a new ability every reincarnation that I get to use just once, a little common courtesy from my Master."

Ray exclaims fervently, "You come to kill me, DO IT!"

Caine laughs. "Ha ha! Oh, my dear, I'm not here to kill you." He walks over to Ray's mother. "I specifically said a loved one, and didn't specify which."

Ray struggles to break free from the spell. He grunts and groans trying desperately to break free. He watches as Caine touches the middle of his mother's back, conjures dark energy and separates her soul from her body. It glimmers bright in his hands. "Absolutely astounding! It shines like an orb full of light, oh how glorious."

Caine lifts his hand and puts Ray's mom's soul to his lips and sniffs. "Wondrous." He tilts his head back, unhinges his jaw, lifts it to his mouth and swallows it whole.

Ray watches in horror as his mother is murdered in front of him. Caine issues a chilling command. "Now ... listen I really enjoyed my meal for the night, thank you so much for providing your services. Now if you want a tip, I suggest ... you ... follow me." Caine takes off as the dark entrapment fades.

Ray's mother collapses to the floor and the patrons in the mall rush over to help her. "Someone call an ambulance!"

Ray starts to go for her and Qasim grabs him by the shoulder. "No, you go!" Ray looks at Qasim, questioning his reasoning. "I saw exactly what that creep did. GO GET HER SOUL BACK! I'll stay behind with her body, GO!" says Qasim affirming to Ray.

Ray nods and runs out of the mall into the parking lot. He extends his left fist with elemental energy to charge his wristband and change into his suit. He takes off in the air after Caine.

Chapter 12: Down in the Dark

Dontrelle, Ezekiel and Vincent return to the base of operations; Master Hue meets them outside.

"Ah, you all have returned," says Hue with a smile on his face.

"Yeah, we decided if all we came into this thang together, we gonna go out of it together too, honorably," Ezekiel valiantly replies.

"I guess we all had the same idea," says Khalia coming from the base carrying the Crown of Thorns. Dontrelle runs up and hugs Khalia. Despite missing just a day of communication, he realizes he has developed feelings for her and wants to hold her tight before everything takes place.

"Trelle," Khalia questions chuckling, "what's up?"

"Be my girl, whether we make it out of this or we die, be my girlfriend." Khalia smiles, scrunches her nose and hugs him, grabbing his hands. Dontrelle smiles along with her. Viera, witnessing the moment, can't help but smile, thrilled for her friend's newfound connection.

Ezekiel looks around and turns to Hue. "Where Ray at?"

Master Hue, a touch of concern in his voice, replies, "He went to go convene with his mother, I have not heard from him since."

A sudden disturbance in the air catches their attention. Looking up, they see Caine soaring toward Piedmont Park, with Ray hot on his heels.

"Oh no," says Dontrelle, his heart racing.

Ezekiel's urgency echoes through the team: "Let's move!" Their collective resolve drives them to action.

* * *

Caine's arrival at Piedmont Park heralds a dark sense of impending doom. His words drip with anticipation as he mutters, "At last, my long-awaited dreams are on the cusp of realization."

Ray, fueled by a mix of determination and anger, touches down and marches forth with a steely resolve toward Caine. However, Caine, the orchestrator of malevolent schemes, halts Ray's advance with a mere gesture.

"Easy there, little light," Caine sneers, his finger conjuring a sphere of ominous dark energy. "Before the show begins, we must set the stage." With a callous gesture, Caine releases the ball of dark energy, allowing it to seep into the earth below. A haunting silence descends upon the park, shrouding it in an eerie stillness. Suddenly, the ground convulses, unleashing a violent upheaval as sinister crystals emerge from the earth's bowels.

Ray's instincts flare, and he swiftly maneuvers to evade the lethal spikes of dark energy crystals that rent the ground apart, barely escaping their deadly reach. "What are these Caine?!" exclaims Ray confused with the recent addition to the park.

"Behold, my dear 'little light,'" Caine sneers, gesturing grandly toward the malevolent crystals that had torn the once serene park asunder. "These demonic energy crystals serve me as what your generation might call ... charging stations! Each summoning fuels my power, granting me strength with every demonic entity brought forth. Impressive, isn't it?"

Ray surveys the devastated park with a mixture of sadness and resentment before fixing Caine with a scorching glare. "Let's cut to the chase then," he retorts, his voice edged with determination.

Utilizing the pulsating energy of the crystals, Caine effortlessly conjures ten demons into existence, causing Ray to stagger in astonishment as they surge toward him. His instincts kick in, and he engages in a meticulously choreographed dance of combat, swiftly confronting each demonic entity. But as he nears victory, Caine cunningly diverts his attention with a burst of dark energy, allowing the remaining demons to ambush Ray, overwhelming him.

"Aye!" Just as Ray found himself overpowered and under attack, Ezekiel intervened, unleashing a torrent of flames that incinerated the demonic assailants. "Off my bro!" Ezekiel proclaims, rescuing Ray from the onslaught.

Ray, visibly stunned by Zeke's timely intervention, exclaims, "Zeke! You saved me?!"

His relief was short-lived as Ezekiel takes a moment, then delivers an avenging punch to Ray's midsection, earning a dull expression from Ray and a nonchalant shrug from Ezekiel. "Aye, worth a try to get my lick back," he quips.

With the team reuniting and Caine advancing, Master Hue swiftly intervenes, asserting, "You all need to talk, but make it brief." Hue charges headlong into battle against Caine, diverting the villain's attention away from the team to facilitate their discussion.

"Y'all, I'm so sorry, I was wrong to read your minds without asking," exclaims Ray. "And, Zeke, I'm sorry, man, I lost my cool and—"

But Ezekiel swiftly interjects, "Ray bruh, chill. It's all good man."

Khalia chimes in reassuringly, "Yeah, bro, calm down."

Ray looks at the team and begins to tear up.

Ray looks around at the team, his eyes welling up with emotion. Before he can continue, Vincent interjects, cutting through the emotional moment. "No time for that," he asserts firmly.

Gathering his composure, Ray steps forward and discloses, "You're right. He took my mom's soul." The team reacts with shock, but Ray swiftly refocuses them. "No time to dwell on it. Hue's running out of energy," he reveals, noting Caine's maneuver against Master Hue. "We've got it from here, Sensei," Ray declares confidently. "Let's move!" Ray steps back as the team swiftly geared up, brandishing their weapons in readiness.

Caine declares menacingly, "I have grown tired of this nonsense!" Caine, growing weary of the ongoing confrontation, expands his arms wide and summons an entire legion of demon while transforming into his demon form.

Ray takes charge, directing his team, "I'll handle Caine. You all deal with the demons. Dontrelle, you're in charge," he appoints, instilling confidence in his fellow Celestial Elementals.

The team assumes combat stances, arming themselves and plunging headlong into the menacing demonic forces. Ray darts skillfully, evading demons and using his staff to fend off a pair before positioning himself directly in front of Caine.

"Shall we, little light?" taunts Caine as he conjures a sword into his hand. Ray charges forward at full speed with his staff, only to be repelled by Caine's swift counter. "I told you, your resolve isn't even enough to begin to defeat me!" Caine boasts.

Ray responds with unflinching determination, "Well I'll make it enough then!" He charges once more, undeterred by Caine's taunts.

In the heat of the battle, Ezekiel, Dontrelle, Vincent, Khalia, and Viera engaged in a frenzied fight against the encroaching demons, wielding their weapons with skill and determination.

"There's twice as many as we faced on the highway," Khalia remarks, her nunchucks expertly disintegrating a demon mid-swing.

Vincent's concern deepens as he points out, "And this time, it's even worse! Look!" The team glances over to witness Caine's crystals, spawning demons and growing in size, looming ominously.

"If this keeps up we'll all be overwhelmed soon," Dontrelle voices, considering their options. "Let's split up and try to clear a path to

Ray!" The team splits up and starts two separate fighting groups.

Khalia and Dontrelle split off together to fight and Vincent, Viera and Ezekiel take off in the opposite direction. Khalia and Dontrelle, fighting seamlessly together, strategically position themselves back-to-back. Khalia seizes an opportunity, releasing a lightning blast that obliterates a wave of demons, creating an opening for Dontrelle. He erects a protective tower around them, unleashing elemental attacks from their vantage point, gaining the upper hand.

Meanwhile, Vincent erects a protective water veil around their group, fortifying their defense. Viera and Ezekiel adeptly wield their weapons, fending off demons attempting to breach their defense. In a momentary distraction, a demon slips behind Ezekiel, but Vincent swiftly intervenes, directing a precise jet stream of water to neutralize the threat just before it strikes.

"Thanks, big bro," Ezekiel says, expressing his gratitude.

"Anytime, lil' bro!" Vincent replies with reassurance.

The group continues their relentless battle, holding their ground against the relentless onslaught of demons, fighting skillfully to pave a way toward Ray's location.

Ray struggles to match Caine's pace, his breaths labored, limbs weary, sweat trickling down his beard as their weapons clash and he is repelled once more.

"Your light is beginning to dwindle, Ray," Caine taunts amid their parries. "Isn't it time to admit your inevitable defeat?"

Through heavy breaths, Ray counters, "As long as my light glows, I won't stop till you're done."

Caine chuckles, his words laced with arrogance. "Ray, you won't be able to save this world, once this is done then I will stake absolute claim to it. I will be king and once I reign, this will be so different. You can be a part of that, Ray, just stop all of this. I'll even release your mother's soul so that she can ascend, just ... surrender."

Ray pauses, weighing Caine's proposition, drawing strength from his valor. "How dare you bargain with my mother's soul?!" Ray surges with elemental energy and charges at Caine with unwavering determination.

Their clash intensifies, but Caine swiftly seizes Ray's staff, wrenching it from his grasp and hurling it away. Ray is thrown off-balance, subjected to consecutive brutal punches that leave him concussed. Then, insult meets injury as Caine flings Ray upside down, gripping him by the ankle.

"I offered you a choice," Caine whispers malevolently as he twists and crushes Ray's ankle before flinging him across the field. Ray cries out in agony, unable to steer his trajectory, the pain of broken bones searing through his body.

Dontrelle and Khalia, witnessing Ray's brutal expulsion, scream out his name in simultaneous anguish.

Chapter 13: Into the Light

Ray's eyes flutter open, finding himself slouched on the church pew, mirroring the past. He attempts to rise, but searing pain seeps through his left leg, pinning him in place. Surveying the empty choir space, he spots an image depicting a river, symbolizing baptism, yet no singers are present. A voice echoes beside him, though no one is there.

"You need to get up, baby. You got a job to do." Ray's mom appears beside him, draped in a white robe. They lock eyes, Ray's filled with confusion. "You have to get up, baby, let that light shine ...Wake up."

Ray awakens with his back against the harsh concrete of the park. He leans up to look out. The rest of the team is struggling to keep up with the demon hordes. Khalia and Dontrelle's pillar has become a tower with Dontrelle trying to fortify it, to keep demons from getting closer as he holds Khalia in his left arm. They are both spent from using their elemental energy to keep the demons at bay.

Vincent is struggling to keep the barrier between the demons, his brother and Viera. Ezekiel and Viera huddle around Vincent to support him. Ezekiel grabs Viera's hand as they all try to use the rest of their strength to fight off the encroaching horde.

Ray attempts to move, yet his strength falters. He tries to heal himself, but his energy is depleted, pain surging throughout his body.

"C'mon, I have to do this. I have to save everything," Ray persists, struggling against his immobilization. "I have to save everyone!"

The fear of failure creeps in on his psyche. He continues to speak, remembering all of what is at stake, "The universe ... the world ... my friends ... my mama ..." Demons surge toward Ray, and his determination heightens. "I have to save 'em, I have to save 'em all."

"I have to save ... I have to save ... myself." The repeated mantra echoes louder, intensifying with each repetition until it transforms into a resounding declaration: "I HAVE TO SAVE MYSELF!"

In that moment, a torrent of elemental energy surges through Ray, enveloping the entire vicinity. It was as if the very essence of the moon had descended upon Earth, taking human form.

Caine's gaze shifts upward in bewildered astonishment, while the team watches in sheer amazement. The demons converging on Ray disintegrate instantaneously. Gradually lifting off the ground, his injured leg heals entirely, and he rises to his feet. As his eyes open, engulfed in a radiant white light, he strides forward, seizing the Crown of Thorns from its sheath. Utilizing it as a conduit, he extracts its properties, infusing them into five luminous energy spheres and into himself. Approaching demons are absorbed into the colossal energy, vanishing into brilliance.

Elevated by the overarching energy, Ray finds its power overwhelming. To contain it, he must release it. Arms outstretched, he disperses the energy spheres among his friends, boosting their own strength and obliterating a wave of nearby demons. Rejuvenated by Ray's shared might, they prepare for battle once more. Ray's irises, initially awash with white light, gradually transition to rotating white circles, indicating the sustained strength within him.

Ray strides back toward Caine, using telepathy to urge his friends to continue fighting and summons his staff into his grasp. Caine summons two successive waves of demons to assail Ray. Swiftly advancing, Ray wields his staff and harnesses his light energy to repel both waves. Then, phasing out of Caine's view, he strikes. Caine attempts a counter, but this time, Ray doesn't recoil. Standing firm, their weapons clash as they confront each other head-on.

Ray's smirk widens as Caine's eyes widen in astonishment. The unlocked power within Ray leaves Caine in sheer awe. Signaling the team to reorganize, Ray employs telepathy to direct Khalia, Vincent, and Viera to merge their elemental energies, while instructing Ezekiel and Dontrelle to do the same. This fusion produces a potent hurricane, combining Khalia's lightning, Viera's air attacks, and Vincent's water manipulations. Simultaneously, Dontrelle and Ezekiel conjure a tempest of magma.

Focused intently on Caine, Ray engages him head-on. They clash without end, exchanging precise strikes, Ray displaying remarkable precision in every move. As Caine attempts to overpower Ray with a strike, both their weapons are dislodged by the recoil. Seizing the opportunity, Caine tries a surprise punch, but Ray meets it head-on, creating a resounding shockwave that visibly rattles Caine.

Undeterred, Ray persists in the hand-to-hand duel with Caine. With evident concern, Caine demands, "How?! How have you amassed such strength? Tell me now!"

Ray retorts forming a fist, "What's the matter, Caine? Weren't you the one pushing me to find my 'resolve'?!" His punch connects, propelling Caine backward. Growing increasingly frustrated, Caine charges at Ray unexpectedly, aiming to deprive him of air by thrusting him into the exosphere. However, despite Caine's onslaught of punches, Ray manages to break free. With astounding speed, he launches a barrage of punches, each weakening Caine further.

Unleashing another surge of energy, Ray propels Caine back to the Earth's surface. Darting into the trees around the park, Ray signals the team to swiftly conclude the battle and follow his lead. He envelops his body in radiant energy, hurtles toward Caine, shattering the sound barrier, and propels Caine to the summit of Stone Mountain. Upon reaching the mountain's pinnacle, he forcefully hurls Caine to the opposite side of the cliff, striding toward him to resume the confrontation.

Meanwhile, the rest of the team relentlessly battles on. Exploiting Caine's absence and the dwindling demon presence, they unleash a coordinated explosion of elemental energy, annihilating every demon and dark energy crystal in the vicinity. Harnessing their individual elements, they converge to join Ray. Ezekiel employs his fire power for propulsion, Dontrelle utilizes earth to hover, Khalia employs lightning speed, running through the streets of Atlanta, Viera commands the air, and Vincent coats himself in water, effortlessly navigating through the air.

Ray, engaged in a relentless struggle with Caine, uses energy spheres to hold him back. Caine, desperate, cries out, "YOU CAN'T BEAT ME ALONE!"

Ray counters, "Oh, I know that ..." Gesturing behind him, the rest of the team emerges over the horizon! They launch a series of assaults on Caine in succession. Khalia and Vincent strike him with combined water and lightning energy, staggering him. Ezekiel and Dontrelle create searing magma, causing intense damage to Caine's flesh, while Viera manipulates the air, propelling a weakened Caine aloft, struggling to break free from her grasp.

Ray telepathically signals the initiation of the crucifix. Dontrelle employs raw elemental energy to grapple Caine's right leg, triggering Caine's auto body defense to launch a dark energy sphere at breakneck speed. Ray intervenes just in time, countering the attack. Each Elemental member, one by one, joins in restraining Caine, while Ray continuously thwarts his auto body responses. As the energies converge on Ray, he deftly dodges, retaliating with light energy spheres, positioning himself to confront Caine. Charging his hands with elemental energy, Ray advances toward Caine.

With closed eyes, Ray whispers, "Guide me, oh God." He shapes a cross in the air using his light energy, tracing a circle around it, the planetary symbol of Earth. He casts it into the air, harnessing it to master the overwhelming energy within him. A transformation occurs— elongated headband, golden accents adorning his clothed armor, holographic angelic wings on his back—his expression composed and resolute. Caine stares, utterly petrified and bewildered.

Grasping the Crown of Thorns from his holster, Ray charges it with radiant light energy and launches toward Caine. Fully empowering the crown, Ray bellows with great strength, "YOU WANTED TO BE A KING SO BAD?! ADORN YOUR CROWN!" He forcefully slams the Crown of Thorns onto Caine's head, evoking a gut-wrenching scream. A cataclysmic clash of light and dark energies ensues. The souls have been freed, yet Caine's dark energy retaliates forcing the crown back. Ray channels all his elemental strength, exerting every ounce of force to drive the crown firmly onto Caine's head.

In the depths of hell, the Devil, connected to Caine, feels his right arm ablaze. Agonized, he orders two minions to retrieve Caine before his borrowed power vanishes into nothingness.

Meanwhile, Ray nears the completion of the crucifix, filling Caine's body with intense light energy, rendering his screams silent. With determination, Ray declares, "This is where you end!" As the radiant light nears the soles of Caine's feet, the two minions emerge, disrupting the team's balance, sending them reeling near the mountain's edge. Collaborating, they thrust Ray airborne, swaying at the brink, struggling to regain footing.

Opening a portal to hell, the minions hurl Caine's body into its abyss, following suit. Ray attempts to intervene, screaming desperately, but the portal seals shut as he crashes onto the ground, utilizing his elemental energy. Collapsing to his knees with heavy breaths and a heart weighed by resentment, Ray lashes out in frustration, "Dammit!" he exclaims as he punches the unforgiving summit of Stone Mountain.

The team rushes to his side. Ezekiel, concerned, calls out, "Ray!"

Dontrelle checks on him, asking, "Bro, you aight?"

"I'm... fine," Ray responds, albeit with a heavy heart.

Viera inquires, "Ray, what just happened?"

Master Hue arrives through a portal, awestruck, and explains, "That... was Archangel... Only accessible when an Elemental reaches their full potential!"

Ray stands, scanning the surroundings, and queries, "Were all the souls released?"

Khalia affirms, "It seemed that way when you crowned Caine."

Gazing at the moon, Ray murmurs, "I wish I could speak to my mom, to know if she made it..."

Ezekiel's smile breaks the mournfulness. "Well ... turn around and ask her yourself."

Ray turns, seeing his mother's spirit on the opposite side of the mountain. "Mama!" he exclaims, rushing toward her, but his hands pass through her radiant form. Overwhelmed, he tries to speak through tears, "Mama, I am so sorry I—"

Ray's mother interrupts by placing her finger on his lips. "Baby, you saved yo mama, it's all OK," she reassures, looking at him with pride, "Look at my baby, fightin' in the name of the Lord and lookin' mighty good doing it!"

Ray smiles through the tears. "Honey, I am so proud of what you've become and everything you're gonna become. Don't stop fightin' and lovin', you hear me?"

Ray nods in agreement. His mother turns to Master Hue and the team. "Y'all take care of my baby now! You hear me, y'all his family now!" They all nod in unity. "Take care of yourself, Ray. I love you." She reaches out to hug Ray and in an instant, she dissolves into the air.

"I love you too ..." Ray watches as her soul ascends to heaven. With tears on the edge of forming, he remembers that there is work to be done. He takes a deep breath and then turns back to the team to give orders.

"Aight, we got work to do," Ray begins, delegating tasks. Khalia prepares to speak, but Ray interrupts and continues, "Vincent, you and Ezekiel go out into the city and repair any damages to water and steel structures. Khalia and Viera, I need you to go out and survey the skies and roads to make sure everything from the city skyline is clear. If you see any demons, take them out. Dontrelle will stay here with Hue and me. We'll combine our powers and repair the landscape." Everyone nods, understanding their assignments and takes off to survey the city.

Ray addresses Dontrelle, "I want to try something." He gazes at the ground. "Place your hand under mine." Dontrelle steps beside Ray and positions his hand underneath. Ray directs Dontrelle to shut his eyes and employ his elemental energy to connect with the mountain. "Do you feel it?" Ray inquires.

"Yeah," Dontrelle responds.

Expanding upon Dontrelle's energy with his light power, Ray grants him the sensation of holding the entire city in his hands. Overwhelmed, Dontrelle receives assurance from Ray that he'll manage. Ray instructs Dontrelle to mend as much as possible, and Dontrelle sets about repairing the park and other demon-damaged sections of the city. Finishing their work, they both stand back.

Ray exhales deeply, remarking, "Well ... that's great." He gazes at the city lights, a smile gracing his face before turning to Dontrelle. "Hey ... um ... you know what it's like ... to lose your parents, right?" Ray asks earnestly.

Dontrelle nods, "Yeah, happened to me a while back ..."

"Okay, you think you could help me with that," he drops to his knees, overcome by a flood of tears, finally releasing the pent-up emotions over the passing of his mother.

Master Hue and Dontrelle immediately gather around, offering comfort and support to

Ray in his time of need. A tear of empathy drops from Dontrelle's face.

Chapter 14: The Grey Area

One week later ...

Saturday afternoon arrives. In the distance, a graveyard stands solemnly. A mahogany casket rests within a gazebo amid the natural surroundings, adorned by a portrait of Ray's mother placed near a podium for anyone to share memories or reflections. Ray sits with his friends in the front row of the funeral procession. Khalia and Vincent grasp Ray's hands while Ezekiel and Dontrelle stand beside him, their hands on his shoulders. Viera tenderly touches the back of his neck.

Ray stands and walks to the podium to speak. "She was a fun mom. A smart mom. A mother who you could tell almost anything without judgment." Everyone chuckles.

"She made the longest days feel like the shortest problems of your life. She could cook like nobody's business, even with all my skills I'll never be able to make that chocolate cake JUST like she did ... I love you, Mom, and I always will. Thank you for giving me everything I needed, just in the nick of time and thank you for making sure you left me in good hands."

Ray walks back to his seat and his friends rally around him as he cries. The pallbearers gently lower her casket into the grave, accompanied by music.

As the repast nears its end, Qasim joins the group. Dontrelle and Ezekiel greet their frat brother warmly; while Khalia, Vincent, and Viera bid their farewells. Qasim approaches Ray, offering a comforting embrace.

Ray acknowledges, "Man, I never told you thank you for watching over her while I went to 'work.'"

"It's no problem, man, I was happy to help in any way possible. How are you feeling?" Qasim inquires.

"I'm feeling feelings, man," Ray replies with a chuckle, gazing away. "I was able to get a lot from my mom before she passed, so I'm missing her much more than I thought I would."

Qasim looks at Ray with kind eyes and places his hand on his shoulder. "You should be very happy about that, Ray, most folks never get anything like that."

Ray looks up. "Yeah, you're right ... You know it's not too late for you too. Maybe reaching out is all it takes sometimes, maybe it'll pan out for you the way it did for me. Well, without the whole evil monster killing parent thing." They share a chuckle.

"I may just give it a try," Qasim responds.

"Need help with anything?" asks Qasim suddenly.

"Well, I think things are done here." Ray has a thought. "Hey, can you come with me? I need some help with something."

Curious but willing, Qasim follows. "Sure, man."

Ray walks with Qasim to an area of the park and checks to make sure no one is around. "OK, don't freak out when I do this," says Ray, trying to reassure Qasim.

"What are you—," Qasim begins, his eyes widening in amazement as Ray concentrates light energy into his fingers. Ray draws a line in the air, opening a dimensional portal, mimicking Master Hue. Ray smiles and gestures. "Please step through." Despite his apprehension, Qasim smiles and steps in. Ray follows suit.

They both step onto the new area for the training grounds. It's like the area before but Hue had made some modifications to the area including a cliff and an ocean below for ambience and focus. The rest of the team is already there training; they and Master Hue welcome Qasim.

"This is amazing!" exclaims Qasim.

"This is our base of operations," Ray explains as he clutches his fist and changes into his armor and pulls out his staff. "We need some help. We need a liaison, someone who will come in his free time and help us monitor things around the city and the world for demon activity and report to us."

Master Hue jests, "It seems that it's time for me to retire from technology." The team chuckles.

"What do you say?" asks Ray. "I mean it only makes sense since you already know our secret." Ray turns to Ezekiel and smirks.

"Hey, man, c'mon I'm trying to do better," replies an embarrassed Ezekiel.

Ray chuckles. "So what do you say?" Qasim thinks for a moment before nodding, and they all smile. Khalia grabs Qasim's arm playfully. "Alright, big bro number two! Let's go into the base and show you everything you've got to get acquainted with."

Ray walks over to Master Hue. Ray bows respectfully, and Hue grasps Ray's hands. "I don't know how I will EVER thank you, for what you have done for the world and the sacrifice it took to get it. What you have accomplished is a success, that no other Elemental of Light has EVER accomplished before in history."

Ray laments, "It's not a real success, to me; it would have been one if my mom was still here."

Hue looks at Ray and smiles. "Your mother's words and her sacrifice, led you to unlock your greatest potential." Hue continues, "It has allowed you to restore the balance back to an even playing field for the side of good. The changes are slowly happening, but the world is healing."

Ray, recalling something, adds, "Caine might return soon. I don't know if that power will return or even if it's still within me."

Master Hue smiles knowingly. Khalia returns with Qasim. Ray addresses the team, "Y'all, I know that at some point, Caine is gonna come back... I think we should train every day; become the best team we can be. I think we can defeat him, once and for all!"

The team raises their weapons in agreement.

Ray begins sparring with Ezekiel. "You ready this time?"

Ezekiel, fists ignited, responds, "Only one way to find out!" The team starts sparring as Ray pauses to gaze at the sunset, the light in his irises returning—a sign that the power he once wielded is still within, dormant until it's needed again.

Made in the USA
Columbia, SC
16 June 2025